finn

a novel

* * *

Matthew Olshan

bancroft
press

Baltimore, MD

Published by Bancroft Press
P.O. Box 65360, Baltimore, MD 21209
800.637.7377
www.bancroftpress.com

Cover design and illustration by Steven Parke, What? Design, www.what-design.com

Book design by Theresa Williams, theresa@visuallee.com

Library of Congress Card Number: 2001086370

ISBN 1-890862-14-2
Printed in the United States of America
First Edition

for shana

"Angry *angry angry*, is what you are," they tell me, but I think I'm less angry than quiet, the kind of quiet that makes people nervous because they can't tell what you're thinking, and most of them assume the worst. I do get angry sometimes, but who doesn't? There's strength in anger, which goes against what school counselors will tell you.

Since I've been living with my grandparents, I'm a lot less angry, but I'm still pretty quiet. My grandparents go on and on about how lovely I am—which I'm not—and how bright—which I'm definitely not. They give me an allowance, which is something new, and nice clothes. Sometimes, when they're showing me off to their wrinkly friends, I feel like saying, "She pees when you give her a bottle!" like those talking dolls they gave me when I first came to live with them, before they understood I was way past dolls.

Still, I like how quiet their house is. I like that there are always clean sheets, even if they do smell like mothballs. Everything in my grandparents' house smells like mothballs, even them sometimes, but it's not a terrible smell. At least it smells like someone's trying. And there are times, late at night, when the smell of the mothballs and the clean sheets and the glow of the stupid little nightlight they insist I need and the cicadas singing outside—when all of it together makes me feel like I'm in a cocoon, like I could become something very nice.

I'll fall asleep with those thoughts sometimes, and even if I haven't had the nightmares, in the morning I'll be lashed down by the sheets. It's the way my grandmother tucks them in. They twist around your ankles like ropes. Come morning, I'll try to hide the fact that I'm in one of my moods, but by now my grandparents know better. When I plop down at the kitchen table, they'll give each other the look that says, "Watch out." They won't bother being cheerful. My grandfather will say, "Another bad night." He's right just to say it and not to ask it, because those mornings, I can barely keep my eyes open, much less answer questions.

They used to try to force me to talk about "it," whatever "it" was. But forcing someone to talk is like forcing them to eat: you may have to break their jaw to do it, and the whole thing can land you in a hospital.

They've been sending me to a girls school called Field, which is supposed to be different from other schools in that you go on a lot of field trips. At first, I liked it. The teachers weren't always making me empty my pockets, and I could go to the bathroom without an act of Congress. My main teacher, Ms. Bellows, was extra nice to me, and not in a condescending way. She was the only one who bothered to call me "Chlo," the way I like, and not "Chloe," with two syllables and the ugly "ee" sound at the end, which is my actual name. The rest of the teachers insisted on the whole ugly thing.

Ms. Bellows understood the kind of nice that being nice is supposed to be about. Most of the other teachers practiced the kind of nice where you've heard a lot of bad stories about someone and think you have to be their "special buddy."

One of the teachers at Field, Mr. Lynch, tried way too hard to be my special buddy, always coming up to me, even when I was with a crowd. It was completely inappropriate. He'd say things like, "Hey, girlfriend!" or "Like those shoes!" It's not impossible that my shoes were nice, or that Mr. Lynch could have genuinely liked them, but the time to compliment them is definitely not when I'm trying to make new friends. Nothing scares away potential friends like a teacher who's complimenting you all the time. It's suspicious.

Mr. Lynch was getting out of hand, so I decided to do something about it. A golden opportunity came one day when he was showing me pictures of his family—that's how much he wanted me to feel like his special pal!—and I saw that his wife was Mexican and very young. She was okay-looking, in that stubby way. You know: too much make-up, not a lot of neck. I don't have anything against Mexicans in general, although a lot of people around here do, but I wanted to get Mr. Lynch off my back, so I started making some seemingly harmless comments about his wife. Such as: wasn't she exotic looking, how long had they been married, etc. Mr. Lynch said that he and Mrs. Lynch were practically newlyweds in that they were about to celebrate their second anniversary.

As soon as I heard that, I had my in. Mr. Lynch is not what you would call a young man, although the fact that he's fat makes his face look pretty young. Unless I'm utterly wrong, he's forty. A man his age should have been celebrating at least his tenth anniversary, if not more.

I congratulated him anyway. I told him I thought that two years of marriage was a *fan-tas-*tic achievement. It wasn't hard to lie to him. Mr. Lynch is the kind of person who sops up compliments, probably because he doesn't feel he really deserves them.

Then, when I was sure he was feeling like my special buddy, I told him—not in a mean way, just as a sort of casual observation—that I was surprised Mrs. Lynch hadn't divorced him yet. Mr. Lynch was a little shocked by that. He asked me why I would say such a thing. I said it was common knowledge that Mexican women married American men to become citizens, and then divorced them later because they find American men fat and not very accomplished lovers.

Mr. Lynch was deeply offended, although I wasn't sure whether it was more what I said about his being unaccomplished or what I said about his being fat. Of course it was both, but I take a sort of clinical interest in insults. I like to know exactly what works, and how well.

Mr. Lynch put his pictures away and got a little pompous, which didn't surprise me. He said, "I assure you that's not the case in our situation." When I heard him use the word "situation," I knew I had struck a nerve, because no one uses a word like "situation" unless they're trying to hide something.

Mr. Lynch was a lot less friendly after that, which suited me fine, because I was trying to be friends with an interesting girl called Marian Williams, who absolutely hated him. She claimed it was an old grudge, but beyond that, Marian was very secretive about her hatred for Mr. Lynch. At first, she would only say that once upon a time Mr. Lynch had betrayed a sacred trust. Marian's always using phrases like "betrayed a sacred trust," which sound ridiculous when I say them, but which somehow sound normal coming from her.

Marian's not very popular. She's one of those people who doesn't care at all what other people think. Unlike me. Personally, I can't *not* care what other people think, no matter how hard I try, but Marian really doesn't, and I mean *really*. Half the time she's in her own little world, so she barely notices that other people even exist.

Marian reads a lot. Too much, judging from the way she lives life in terms of books. For instance, the business with Mr. Lynch. I finally got it out of her that the "sacred trust" Mr. Lynch betrayed was that he had voted, along with several other teachers at Field, to remove *The Adventures of Huckleberry Finn* from the summer reading list. Apparently, there's a lot of offensive language in the book, and it's racist. Marian almost took off my head when I mentioned that. She said that only people who hadn't read the book at all—at least not the way Mark Twain intended it—could call it "racist." I tried to point out that no one really knows how Mark Twain intended it, and we weren't ever likely to, since he was dead, but that's just the kind of argument you can't win with Marian, because suddenly, instead of talking about Mark Twain, you're talking about Genghis Kahn or the Holocaust, and how can you argue with that?

Anyway, after Mr. Lynch voted the way he did about *Huckleberry Finn*, Marian made a big show of avoiding him in the hallways, flattening herself against the lockers when he walked by, making the sign of the cross behind his back. She was like a bad vampire movie. Once, after a big snowstorm, she spent half an hour in the parking lot carving some crazy footprints in the snow by his car. It was classic Marian. She said she was sculpting the footprints of Huck Finn's murderous father. "In the book, the left boot heel had a cross in it," she said. "To ward off the devil." She's a real stickler for accuracy.

Mr. Lynch was supposed to recognize the footprints and interpret them as a threat. When I asked, "What kind of threat?" Marian rolled her eyes at me, the way she does whenever she thinks someone's being hopelessly thick, which in my case is fairly often. "The Vengeful Cry of the Oppressed," she said. "Duh!"

Carving the footprints was a lot harder than she originally thought, because it's not exactly easy to avoid leaving your own footprints in the snow, not to mention the occasional handprint when you lose your balance. In the end, it looked to me as if a big hairy dog had jumped out of Mr. Lynch's car and rolled around, but Marian was satisfied that the Oppressor was in for a real scare. I was glad to hear that because, by then, I thought I was going to chip a tooth from shivering so hard.

We watched Mr. Lynch get into his car that afternoon, and, in fact, he did pause for a while after he squeezed himself behind the wheel, but I had seen him do that before. He's just extremely out of shape and he fiddles with the radio for a minute to catch his breath before he straps on his seatbelt, because reaching over his shoulder is a big workout for him. But in Marian's mind, Mr. Lynch wasn't catching his breath at all. "He's contemplating the Harvest of his Cowardice!" she said.

The harvest of his cowardice? I mean, *please*.

chapter two

My grandparents have decided to kick out the maid, a really nice Mexican woman called Silvia. Lots of their friends have Mexican maids. It's what people do around here, but I always thought that if I had to be a Mexican maid, I'd want to work for my grandparents, since they aren't particularly mean, or if they are sometimes, it's so obviously because of how they were brought up that I wouldn't take it too personally. I always thought that my grandparents were different, but that was before what they did to Silvia.

I had known for a long time that Silvia was pregnant. It was pretty obvious, unless, like my grandmother, you refused to have unpleasant thoughts. Actually, my grandmother did notice something. One day, while Silvia was putting away the groceries, my grandmother pointed out how Silvia's shirt kept riding up. Silvia must have been five months along by then. Her belly button was already pooching out. But instead of thinking that Silvia could be pregnant, my grandmother called up the appliance repairman to come out and look at the dryer. She thought it might be running too hot and making Silvia's shirts shrink.

Calling a repairman because you're worried about ruining the maid's wardrobe is actually pretty nice, and I admired my grandmother for it, even if it did showcase her stubborn mind. My grandfather, on the other hand, was noticing Silvia more and more, and not in a nice way. He was always complimenting her, pointing out how rosy her cheeks were, or what a fine figure she was developing. He asked her if she wasn't eating too much pasta. For some reason, my grandfather thinks that "Silvia's people" are crazy for pasta. That's how much he knows about Mexicans.

Silvia was living in my grandparents' basement when I came to live with them. I didn't see much of her at first. I had a lot on my mind and kept pretty much to myself, but beyond that, Silvia really seemed to want to be invisible. You barely knew she was around, which was just how my grandparents liked it. I might not have gotten to know her at all if I hadn't offended my grandfather at the Navy Gravy.

At the time, my grandparents were going out of their way to include me in lots of "family time." At least, that's the reason they gave for never leaving me alone. It sounds callous, my not wanting to spend time at home with them. I just couldn't stand the way they floated around the house like jellyfish. I was constantly like: *hurry up!*

Even going out with them was claustrophobic. They liked to get dressed up and take me out to eat. There was one seafood place they liked in particular, the Navy Gravy. It had tables with fake "pieces of eight" under the varnish. The manager wore a pirate patch. He was short and oily and acted like a funeral director, except that his hands were constantly on the waitresses, inspecting them, straightening a name tag, puffing up a frilly white collar. He liked to say things like, "Swab that deck, wench!" when a table needed clearing. The waitresses liked to mock him behind his back.

We went there for the crabs. My grandfather loved smashing crab claws with his wooden mallet and digging his thumbs into the crunchy bodies. He'd suck the juice out of the tiny side legs, then toss them in a revolting heap right on the table. My grandmother and I always finished eating about an hour before my grandfather. Then we had to just sit there, trapped in the booth like hostages, and watch the carnage.

My grandfather would hammer away. Every once in a while, my grandmother would ask him if the crabs were sweet. The answer was always, "Not as good as last time." He had a way of making everything sound like her fault.

One night, I finally reached my limit. While we were waiting for the umpteenth platter of crabs, I asked my grandfather if he knew what crabs ate. His hammer stopped in mid-air.

"Crabs, you mean the animal?" he said. "You're asking, 'What do they eat for food?'"

"Right," I said.

"In the wild? I don't know. Fish eggs. Tiny shrimp, maybe. Kelp."

"Say, I know," my grandmother said brightly. "Those itty bitty dots that whales eat. What's that called? They're like miniature snowflakes—"

"You mean plankton," I said.

"Plankton. Good for you!" she said. "I think I read that somewhere." She was so happy that we were having a family conversation. I almost hated to ruin it. "Nope," I said.

"All right, Miss Smartypants," my grandfather said. "Enlighten us."

"Crabs," I said, "are scavengers. Like the vulture. Or the common sewer rat."

"Eskimo," my grandmother said, darting her wet eyes at my grandfather. "Eskimo" was their code word for, "Time to change the subject."

"They taught us that at Field," I said. "Matter of fact, what the crab *really* likes, even more than fish eggs or the occasional miniature shrimp, is medical waste. It's like a delicacy to them. Particularly used bandages. Crusty gauze."

This was actually something I'd heard about lobsters, but I didn't put that kind of behavior past a crab, either.

"Chloe!" my grandmother said.

"Well, it's true!" I said. "We learned it in Ecosystems."

My grandfather looked at my grandmother accusingly. "That would be our cue to leave," he said. Then he took a long drink of water and started cleaning his gory fingers with a Wet-Nap.

After that, I didn't have to go to the Navy Gravy with them, which was great, because they'd leave money for Silvia and me to order a pizza and have a "girl's night in."

That's how I first got to know Silvia. She was nice enough, but pretty ignorant. She was easy to tease, especially about electronics. I guess Mexicans don't own a lot of the things we take for granted. Or maybe they do, but the instructions all come in English.

Take the television, for instance. One night, I convinced Silvia that the TV was leaking radiation. I went to the bathroom and brushed my gums until they bled. Then I went behind the TV and put my hands on it and said, "Oh my God!" When Silvia asked me what I was doing, I told her I thought something was wrong with the TV. Then I made a big point of "discovering" my bloody gums. I could tell she was getting good and nervous. I think she was afraid that my grandparents would blame her for my bleeding gums. She came over to take a closer look, but I said, "My mouth can wait." I held her hand to the back of the television. "You feel that?" I said.

"I don't feel it," she said, which was pretty funny because she didn't even know what she was supposed to be feeling yet.

"Yes you do," I said. "The heat. Televisions are supposed to be cold inside, like refrigerators." Silvia nodded and tried to pull her hand away, but I kept it there. "It's hot," I said. "And that can only mean one thing. Radiation! Which would explain the bleeding gums."

Silvia managed to stay fairly calm until I told her to call 9-1-1. I knew she wouldn't. She's an illegal alien and paranoid of the police. Instead, she ran to the kitchen and brought me some ice for my gums, which was very sweet of her. Then she told me to take off all my clothes and get in the shower to wash off the radiation. The shower idea was too much. I mean, a shower. What a simpleton!

When she found out I had fooled her, she was pissed—particularly about the 9-1-1 business—but it didn't last long. Silvia couldn't hold a grudge. Besides, I had seen her boyfriend Roberto sneaking into her room a bunch of times, and she knew I had seen him. With something like that on her, I could pretty much do whatever I wanted.

Truth was, I never would have ratted her out about Roberto, even if I didn't approve of all the sneaking around, which I didn't. It wasn't as if he was repulsive. I suppose you could even call him handsome, in a South of the Border way, if you didn't mind the odd gold tooth or the armfuls of cheap stuffed animals that came with the package. Silvia liked him plenty. They were always smooching and doing more than that when they thought I wasn't looking. I'm the first to stand up for people's privacy, but the way Silvia and Roberto went at it, sometimes I wondered if they wanted to get caught.

One morning, I saw that Silvia's eyes were puffy and red, and her cheeks, which were plump to begin with, were all swollen. I asked her if she was okay and she gave me a long hug, squeezing much too hard, the way people do when they're very upset, and she said, "Oh, Chica"—that's what she called me when she was feeling particularly tender—"my Roberto is moving to California for his job. I am to be all alone." Silvia could be very dramatic. I told her that she still had me, and not to worry, because she could save up her money and go out and visit him.

That's when I learned something awful about my grandparents. They weren't paying her! Silvia told me that my grandparents were giving her "room and food," which meant a lousy basement apartment and a few bags of groceries each week. And they promised not to call Immigration on her. In exchange, Silvia worked twelve hours a day, six days a week.

I confronted my grandfather about it because he's notoriously cheap. I figured the arrangement had to be his idea, but he surprised me by saying that my grandmother was the one who "handled the girl." When I asked my grandmother about it, she got all testy and told me I shouldn't poke around in Silvia's business. I told her it wasn't Silvia's business I was interested in. I just wanted to know what made someone think they could make another person work so hard without paying her. That's when my grandmother said, "Silvia's situation is none of your business."

I might have let that go if she hadn't used the word "situation." I never knew until that moment that my grandmother was hiding things from me. I thought she was bigger than that.

Silvia found out she was pregnant two weeks later. I helped her with the test. She couldn't read the instructions in the box. In her defense, the print was pretty tiny, but I'm not sure she'd have been able to understand them, even if they were in Spanish. I told her what to do while she did the test, peeing into a cup and then testing her pee with a plastic wand. If she wasn't pregnant, we were supposed to see a minus sign; if she was, we'd see a plus sign. I didn't get into that with her, because I wasn't sure how strong she was in math.

It turns out I didn't have to explain a thing. A plus sign showed up, which of course Silvia interpreted as a cross—she's extremely Catholic, not to mention superstitious. She whispered, "Dio mio!" and then she tried to faint, but the bathroom was too small, so all she managed to do was slump down over the toilet. It was funny to watch, but I didn't laugh because I knew that underneath all the dramatics, Silvia's life was suddenly a lot more complicated.

She made me swear not to tell my grandparents. Then she told me some more awful things about them, like what they said about Mexican girls the first time she met them. By now she was sitting on the toilet, rocking back and forth, shaking the pregnancy test like a thermometer, as if she wanted to take it again, just to be sure. "They told me not have any boyfriends, because Mexican girls like to have too many babies," she said. Apparently, my grandfather also said some very rude things about Mexican girls who sneak into the States just to have a baby here, so it can be a U.S. citizen. That part didn't surprise me too much. I had heard it before. I had even modified it slightly and used it with Mr. Lynch. But my grandfather went on to say that Mexican girls who did that were no better than animals, and any self-respecting citizen had a moral obligation to send a pregnant Mexican back home to Mexico, where she belonged. So Silvia knew what was in store for her if my grandparents found out.

And they might not have found out, if it hadn't been for me. Silvia got very good at hiding the pregnancy. She wore baggy clothes and all sorts of underwear contraptions, and it's extremely possible that she could have hidden the whole thing from my grandparents, right up to the birth. In the final weeks of her pregnancy, I had been picking up some of the slack, things that Silvia just couldn't do, like scrubbing the floors and putting the high dishes away. My grandmother asked me if I had seen Silvia eating a lot of sweets lately, but otherwise she didn't seem to suspect a thing. Silvia had a plan for having the baby, which she didn't tell me much about, but apparently it had something to do with people from her church.

This is something that's hard for me to talk about. It still makes me sick to think I did it, but I was really angry at Silvia because she wouldn't take me out driving. My grandparents had two cars, a fancy one and an everyday one. So when they ran an errand, or went to one of their thousands of doctors' appointments, the fancy one just sat in the garage. That seemed like a waste, so I was making Silvia teach me how to drive. I won't be legal for a few years, but I'm tall and athletic for my age, and I look a lot older, and driving is something I really like to do. If I came home early from school and my grandparents were out on an errand, I'd make Silvia drive us over to the Safeway parking lot. When we got there, Silvia would slide over and fasten her seatbelt and I would walk around to the driver's side and adjust the seat, since I'm a lot taller than she is. I'd practice driving, mostly in circles. I'd make the tires squeal a few times, just to watch the expression on Silvia's face. She hated driving with me, but most of the time she couldn't refuse, on account of what I knew about her and Roberto.

Until two days ago. It was late in the afternoon. My grandparents had gone out to fill a bunch of prescriptions. I told Silvia to take me driving. Silvia said no. She said that driving the car made her nervous for the baby. She said she could get sent back to Mexico for driving without a license, and besides, she didn't like lying to my grandparents.

I don't know what I was thinking. I'd been having the same nightmare for a week, the one where I'm in the hospital giving birth, and I see the baby coming out, but instead of a baby, it's my mother's head. In the dream, the head glares at me and then starts gnawing on the umbilical cord. That's when I usually wake up.

So I was practically a zombie from lack of sleep. That's no excuse, and I'm really ashamed of it now, but I lashed out. I told Silvia she had to do what I said or else I'd tell my grandparents how she was lying to them every day, and that the biggest lie of all was the little brown bastard in her belly. Silvia looked horrified, more horrified than she should have been, even at my saying something like that. "Chica," she said softly, "look who's home." And there they were, frozen in the doorway with their big prescription bags from the drug store. I'd been so worked up that I hadn't heard them come in. Their eyes were focused like lasers on Silvia's belly. My grandmother moved behind me and clamped her hands on my shoulders and said, "Oh, Silvia. How could you?" My grandfather waved us away and said, "I'll handle this."

My grandmother took me to my room, and we sat down on the edge of the bed until my grandfather came to get us. We didn't talk much while we were waiting. My grandmother kept saying, "It's just a shame, that's all. She'll be fine. Just fine." Meaning back home in Mexico.

Yesterday morning, Silvia left. My grandfather made a thorough inspection of the basement apartment to see if Silvia had stolen anything. My grandmother waited for him at the kitchen table, stirring her decaffeinated tea and telling me I should learn my lesson from this, that you can never trust "those people," not even the girls. "Well?" she said, when my grandfather finally came upstairs to make his report.

"I didn't notice anything missing, but that doesn't mean she didn't steal."

"Did she leave a mess?"

"No. It's clean. She left some of her religious garbage in the bathroom. But otherwise, no."

"Oh," said my grandmother. She seemed disappointed.

If the whole thing hadn't been my fault, I would have been furious with her.

chapter three

I guess I'm through with sleeping. Ever since I got Silvia fired, I can't seem to keep my eyes closed. I tell myself that it's her fault for getting pregnant. And for being illegal to begin with. But whatever she did wrong still doesn't justify what I did wrong. That's a rule my father—rest in peace—taught me.

This morning at school, I must have looked awful because Ms. Bellows came up to me after first period and asked me if I needed to lie down. I said no, not really. I almost told her about Silvia, but then I didn't, because I knew that telling her would make me feel better. I didn't want to feel better, at least not yet. Ms. Bellows said that I should try to get some fresh air—they're very big on fresh air at the Field School—and I said okay, because I really was having trouble keeping my head off my desk.

I went outside for a while, but the sound of the younger girls playing depressed me, so I went back in to find Marian. I found her in science lab, off in a corner by herself, as usual, roasting the cap of her ballpoint pen over a Bunsen burner. I had to hand it to her—she looked great, even in a white lab coat. She was wearing a pair of antique safety goggles that made her look like Marie Curie. Little details like the antique goggles made me believe the rumors I'd heard about her being rich.

Marian almost blew it by saying, "Why, Chloe! What a lovely surprise," as if I had just walked into her kitchen. I told the science teacher that the principal had an urgent message for Marian. He went out of his way to believe me. The Field School likes to make its students feel like "Responsible Citizens."

Marian and I went up to the Hollow, our hangout at the high end of the school grounds. To get there, you follow a dirt path behind some boxwoods to a little nook. The ground there is dry and covered in pine needles. The hedges form a nice thick wall between you and the school. But the best part about the Hollow is the gap in the chain link fence. You could squeeze through it, if you wanted to, and be right out on the sidewalk. Free as a bird. Marian and I hadn't done that yet—we preferred to lean back against the gnarled roots of the hedges and people-watch—but the possibility of escape made the place feel extra secret.

I thought it was going to be hard to tell her about Silvia, but even before we were settled in, I was blurting everything out like a baboon. Marian sat there, outlining her lips with a knuckle, as if she were applying my story like lipstick. When she finally said something, she sounded almost like a normal person—a very rare phenomenon, I can assure you. She was at her most serious.

"Chlo," she murmured, "you have to fix this." I knew she was right, but I wasn't ready to admit it. I pointed out that Silvia wasn't exactly innocent, since she had started the whole thing by: a) being illegal and b) getting herself pregnant.

"She couldn't help it," Marian said. "Latins are hot-blooded." I waited for more, but Marian was laying it on pretty thick with all the silence. Finally, she asked me what my intentions were. I said I was still working on them. She told me not to think about it too long, because the streets could be very cruel. "You've read Dickens?" she asked.

I resented the Dickens comment, because, in fact, I had read some

Dickens, and I knew that horrible things always happened to the characters in his books when they got booted out, even if everything worked out in the end.

Marian could tell I was annoyed. "I think you need some time alone with your thoughts," she said.

"Whatever," I said.

"*Ciao, bella,*" she said. Then she put on her Marie Curie goggles and left.

I sat and sulked in the Hollow for a while. I wondered how long it would be before Ms. Bellows started to worry about me. I imagined what it would be like if first Ms. Bellows, and then everyone else, one by one, deleted my existence from their minds. It was a perfect, melancholy thought. I lay back. The hedges waved their stiff arms over me. The sun lit up the veins in the fluttering leaves. The occasional jet sliced silently through the high clouds. Sleep was finally catching up.

I must have rolled a little during my nap, because when I woke up, my feet were where my head had been. My face was full of sun. A man was shouting at me, but the more I woke up, the quieter his voice got, until it was almost like a whisper, as if I was a baby and he had moved me to my crib and was trying to talk me back to sleep. The man was standing over me, whispering. He wore a wool hat, which was out of place because it was May and already warm. He was big and fat and he had one of those tiny triangular beards on his chin that they call a "soul patch." In my groggy state, I imagined that he was freeing my arms, which seemed to be tangled in the gap in the fence. But then the metal bit into my arm, and the pain woke me up completely and I realized he wasn't freeing me from the fence at all.

He was dragging me through it.

chapter four

* * *
* *

I flailed my arms and legs and screamed "Rape!", which was what I thought you were supposed to do when a strange man was grabbing you, but there were only two people nearby, a bicycle courier with dreadlocks sitting on the sidewalk next to his bike, and a businesswoman clopping along in high heels and a fancy suit. The bicycle courier was watching what was happening very closely, and even though he didn't get up to help, I at least got the feeling he considered it, unlike the businesswoman, who looked at her watch, pretended to remember something important, and took off across the street. I could almost forgive the bicycle courier. I'll bet his legs were aching and this could have been his only chance to rest all day. But the businesswoman really bothered me, not so much for being a coward, which was understandable, but for that phony glance at her watch. What a hypocrite!

Soul Patch wasn't helping my case by shouting "Come on, Chloe, now stop it!" at the top of his lungs. Strange as it may seem, I wasn't too surprised he knew my name. After all, he had touched me while I was sleeping, which was so intimate. Soul Patch was saying other things which struck me as truly bizarre, like, "Haven't we talked about this?" and "Is this how I taught you to behave?" as if we were having a conversation. No—as if I was *family*. I suppose it made good sense for him to say those things—strictly from the point of view of a kidnapper—because it gave people like the bicycle courier or the cowardly businesswoman the excuse they needed not to get involved. It helped them imagine that my screaming "Rape!" and flailing around were things that a spoiled brat would do to embarrass her father—who, when I finally admitted it to myself, was the person that Soul Patch was most trying to sound like.

The fact that he was trying to sound like my father really set me off, because if I made a list of the people I loved most in the world, my father would occupy the number one spot, even though he's been dead for a long time. And to have someone as disgusting as Soul Patch pretend to be my father while snatching me out of school and forcing me into a big van painted up with barbarian women in bikinis—let's just say it gave me a new burst of energy.

Soul Patch quietly apologized as he clamped his sweaty hand over my mouth. He was wearing one of those fingerless gloves that bicyclists wear. I was glad of it, too, because even though the leather was damp and a little rank, I imagined that the palms of his hands were a thousand times worse. He was being very formal for some reason, asking me to please watch my head as I stepped up on the van's running board, and, after we were inside, wondering if the duct tape was too tight as he wrapped it around my hands. He apologized for it being so hot in the back of the van, since most vans didn't have air conditioning, at least not for the cargo area, and his van didn't have any at all, not even for the driver. The formality didn't exactly make me feel comfortable, but at least I wasn't quite so scared when he climbed back out and slid the side door shut. He said, "Watch yourself, now," as he slammed it, which struck me as funny. It was something a soccer Mom would say.

The van had a metal mesh wall blocking off the cargo area, so I couldn't do very much in the way of eye-scratching, ear-biting, or crotch-pounding, which were three other things I heard were good in a crisis. Soul Patch strapped on his seatbelt and brushed his sweaty hair straight back with the tips of his thumb and forefinger—he was strangely careful about keeping the bicycle glove away from his hair, as if he had heard that human hair sweat destroys even a good pair of bicycling gloves—and then, when he was all strapped in, he heaved a big sigh, as if we had both just narrowly escaped an ambush, and said, "So, are we all set?"

He seemed to be asking the question as much for himself as for me, but I answered by holding up my arms, so he could see the long red curves where the fence had scratched me. I guess he had been focused on trussing me up, because he was genuinely surprised to see the blood. The cuts were pretty shallow, so it's possible that they hadn't started bleeding when he was taping me up. Now, though, there were some nice thick red lines—no big deal, really. I've had a lot worse. Still, I thought he was going to pass out when he saw it.

He said, "Oh, *man!*" His head drooped as if he was going to put it between his legs, the way you do to avoid fainting. I couldn't be sure, but it was completely possible that the sight of the blood on my arms actually did make him feel faint. That's how totally *not* threatening he was. When he squeezed the bridge of his nose, the Velcro flaps of the bicycle gloves—he didn't fasten them, I think, because his hands were too fat—brushed his unshaven cheeks and made a scritching sound. Then he turned to me. "You're okay, right?" he said. "I mean, you're not going to need stitches, are you?"

I shrugged, although it was completely obvious that I didn't need them.

Soul Patch slammed the steering wheel. The padding in the palm of his gloves absorbed most of the force and made a little squeaky noise, like a bath toy, which irritated him even more because even his angry gesture was a flop. "That's just what I need," he said. "Your mother's going to *freak.*" Then he turned off his hazards, signaled with his left blinker—he was such a careful driver!—and pulled slowly away from the curb, driving gently, as if I was fragile cargo.

It all made sense as soon as he mentioned my mother, but the fact that she was involved was quite serious. She wasn't supposed to come near me any more, at least not according to the judge's order. I would have been happy if she had just stayed in Texas or wherever and left me alone. As far as I was concerned, the farther away the better.

Even if it had been legal, my mother wouldn't have dared to come see me at my grandparents. They were my Dad's parents, not hers. His parents never liked my Mom, starting from even before they met. They disliked her on principle, because they thought she wasn't good enough for my Dad. They made it hard enough for her when my Dad was still alive, and then, after he was gone, they didn't hold anything back. I can't even count the number of times I've sat at the kitchen table and listened to my grandmother badmouth my Mom. She always calls her "that woman." To this day, I've never heard my grandmother speak my mother's name, which is Claire. "That woman," my grandmother will say, "never lived up to your father's level." Meaning, I suppose, that it's her fault she was born who she was. It's annoying to listen to my grandmother say those things. It makes it a lot harder to respect her as a person if, after all these years, she can't find it in her heart to forgive my mother for what she did. But my grandmother still blames my mother for my father's death. She says that my mother caused it. "By omission, if not commission," she says. I wish she could just let it be. I hate the way she stirs things up.

"So you must be the boyfriend," I said. My voice felt small rattling around in the back of that big van, which was bare inside, no seats or anything. It wasn't exactly comfortable back there, bouncing around on the metal floor. He didn't seem to hear me, so I gave one of my patented folded tongue whistles. You can hear it from about a mile away.

That got his attention. "Oh my God," he said.

"I *said*, 'Are you the boyfriend?'" He laughed at that, which surprised me.

"You make it sound so temporary," he said. "I'm your mother's husband, which I guess makes me your step-dad. But you don't have to call me that right away. I'm Bobby. Sorry about back there. Not a very good first impression."

"You could have invited me over. *Politely,*" I said.

He laughed again. "Now why didn't I think of that?" he said sarcastically. Even his sarcasm was babyish. "I'll try to remember," he said. "For next time."

He was right, of course. Under normal circumstances, I wouldn't have come near him. I told him so, although I think the way I put it was that under normal circumstances I wouldn't come anywhere near such a fat stinking bastard. He even thought that was sort of funny. He kept on laughing until I insulted his soul patch, which seemed to touch a nerve.

After that, he suggested we keep our thoughts to ourselves until we got to where we were going.

chapter five

Who can explain the river of junk that flows through a person's mind? Propped up against the back doors of that rancid van, I should have been thinking of a million things, such as: how to fool Bobby into thinking I was carsick, or what I'd whisper to the police if I managed to sneak a phone call, or how I'd calm down my mother when I saw her. Useful things. But what was I thinking about instead? The sky, which was pretty much all I could see through the bug-splattered windshield, and how blue it looked. Blue, and strangely merciful. I can't really explain why I thought that. I just did. I should have been listening for changes in the road, memorizing the turns we made, studying the branches of trees we passed, for landmarks. Anything but making googly eyes at the clouds like a baby. I swear, sometimes I could shoot myself.

Even with my temporary lapse, I was confident we were still in the city when Bobby finally parked the van. The potholes had been getting worse and worse, which was a sure sign we weren't in the suburbs. Bobby got out and opened the side door for me, bowing like a butler after it slid open and locked in place with a loud thunk. He made a big show of helping me out. I ignored his help, pretending I didn't need it. That was a big mistake. I don't ever recommend jumping with duct tape around your wrists, because you're liable to lose your balance when you land, and by then it's too late to think about how you're going to protect yourself from the ground when you fall, because you can't use your hands much for that, either. I ended up face-down in the gutter. My mouth touched wet garbage.

So I had to accept Bobby's help in the end, anyway, and now I had some new scrapes on my knees and one on my elbow to add to the list. Bobby brushed off my knees, which I resented, because, in my mind, street filth was still a lot cleaner than his fingers. He stayed close to me as we walked down the sidewalk. He was constantly trying to put his arm around me, not because he was feeling particularly friendly, which he hadn't been since the soul patch comment, but because he wanted to hide the fact that my hands were bound together with duct tape. In broad daylight. A girl walking down the street like that in my grandparents' neighborhood would have been surrounded by police before she got ten feet, but no one here seemed to care, or even to notice.

I had never seen this neighborhood before. It was all row houses, tiny narrow identical ones with fake stone siding and pretentious marble steps, all squeezed in together with about two inches of sidewalk in front of them. The row houses looked as if they were all trying to keep from being pushed into the street by someone who thought they were totally hideous. The puny sidewalk was full of white trash bags, which stank like summer garbage. Some of the houses were abandoned, with plywood sheets nailed over fire-blackened window frames. A lot of them had spray-painted signs saying "If animal trapped inside, call…" but there was never a phone number written in. There were no trees anywhere.

The streets were full of people, unlike my grandparents' neighborhood, where you're lucky to see an overweight jogger or a big black nanny out with a blond toddler. Everyone here was black. There were street corner boys dressed up in baggy clothes, waving their long arms and mouthing rap songs. I couldn't tell if they were trying to be funny, or menacing, or both.

Gigantic families clustered on the marble steps, as if a smoke alarm had driven them all out half dressed, eating, in curlers, clutching their pathetic belongings. Some of the old men stood there in their pajamas, smoking. It was so noisy! Babies squalled, their fat mamas shrieked, kids whooped, rap music blared, the passing cars honked their horns, sometimes friendly, sometimes not. Everybody seemed to know everybody else, except for Bobby.

The fact that we were white seemed to make us invisible, which was the opposite of my grandparents' neighborhood, where it's black people who are invisible. Wait, I take that back. It wasn't exactly the opposite. In my grandparents' neighborhood, they just *pretended* that black people were invisible. Black people are actually watched very closely there. But here, in this neighborhood, Bobby and I were barely noticed, or if we were, it was with a knowing look, as if all white people wrapped their children up with duct tape and dragged them down the sidewalk.

There were several men in dreadlocks who actually looked like they knew what to do with a giant heap of knotty hair—unlike the bicycle courier back at Field, who was white and whose dreadlocks were yellowish and scrawny. A squat balding man walked by with something rolled up in a newspaper. He was carrying it at arm's length. His face was turned away, as if what he was carrying really stank. As he passed, I saw a furry little tail poking out of one end of the roll and some whiskers poking out of the other end. I couldn't tell whether it was a kitten or a very large rat. Whatever it was was definitely dead.

"This is us," Bobby said, stepping up to one of the identical steel front doors. It took him a minute to find the key. He had an enormous wad of keys. Most of them looked brand new, as if he had swiped a lot of blanks at the hardware store. He pawed through them, grunting when he found the right one. "Sorry about the mess," he said, kicking the door open with the toe of his boot, which hit the door like a hammer and made a loud clang. There were a lot of black dents in the bottom of the door. The last thing I saw on the street, before we plunged into the steaming atmosphere of the house, was a big sign nailed to the front of a church across the street. It was one of those temporary churches black people set up in storefronts. The sign was shaped like a rocket. Badly painted fire spewed from its engines. The sign said, "Fly with Jesus to the heavens."

"Your mother should be here any minute," Bobby said, bolting the door. Then he told me to make myself comfortable. I said *as if*. The air was putrid and sticky. Bobby started to clear some moldy TV dinners off the sofa. The trays left a dusty outline on the upholstery, which was blue denim. The pillows looked like overstuffed plumber's pants, complete with a butt crack.

I sat down on the stairs by the front door. I kept moving up the stairs, one by one, trying to find the most comfortable height, but then Bobby came over to the banister and told me to please stay in view, so I moved down to the fourth stair. It was still better than sitting on the denim sofa. I've always liked sitting on stairs. It makes me feel like I have options.

Soon, there was banging at the door. I could hear the crinkle of paper shopping bags, which my Mom always insists on—she thinks they're classier than plastic—and her shrill voice cursing Bobby and demanding that he open the damn door because her hands were full. Bobby's thick fingers fumbled with the bolt. He kept saying, "Hold your horses, sweetie." He sounded nervous. He was a big guy, but he was right to be nervous. Mom was capable of anything.

Bobby finally got the door open. Mom came in, cursing him for making her drop one of the bags. She was ready to really lay into him, but then she saw me. She smiled one of those smiles of hers which might have been pretty if you didn't know for sure that there was something bad behind it. "Well, I'll be," she said. "If it isn't my Chlo-worm." "Chlo-worm" was her pet name for me. It came from a rubber worm she gave me that glowed in the dark.

She looked surprised to see me. As if she hadn't sent her pig-faced boyfriend to kidnap me.

I didn't rush up to give her a hug, which seemed to bother her. You wouldn't think a person as shrewd as my Mom was capable of fooling herself about anything—for instance, the idea that after everything she'd done to me, I'd still run over and give her a big sloppy hug. It just goes to show that even very clever people can deceive themselves.

"I take it you've met Bobby," she said. I didn't say anything. I just showed her the cuts on my arms, which looked a lot worse than they felt. I hadn't bothered to clean them up, since I figured the messy scabs would come in handy. Bobby cringed and started to explain, but Mom cut him off, without looking at him, without saying a word, just by snapping her sharp little fingers and pointing at his throat. "I'll deal with that later," she said, in a way that almost made me feel sorry for Bobby, even though he was a grown man. Then she came up to me and tucked my hair behind my ears. She smelled like cigarettes, but not the usual. A new brand.

"You look good," she said. "Your grandparents have been fatten-ing you up."

"Not too much," I said.

"Well, that's all over," Mom said. "You're with us now."

By even talking to me, she was breaking the law, but I knew better than to point that out. A restraining order isn't much help when you're in immediate danger. Instead, I tried to be all innocent. "Is this where we're going to live?" I said.

"What, is there something wrong with it? What'd they do, spoil you? Send you off to finishing school?"

As if she hadn't told Bobby where to find me. "I go to Field School now," I said.

"Field? That's private. Very expensive. A waste of money."

"It's a good school," I said.

"I'll bet it is. Full of fancy teachers and spoiled brats."

"Are we going to live in the city?"

"Listen to you, with your little questions. What ever happened to 'Hey, Mom, long time no see?'"

I didn't say anything, because I knew how bad it was to lie to her.

"That's just what I thought," she said. She turned to Bobby. "You see this? Was I exaggerating?"

Bobby didn't speak, but at least he looked sorry for me, which was potentially useful. Mom had him take me upstairs. "Make sure she's not going anywhere," Mom said. Her bossy tone made Bobby pout.

"I told you already," he said. "I put a padlock on the window."

"Well then, check it," Mom said. "She's been known to jump ship."

Bobby muttered to himself, but only after we were out of earshot. "Here's your new home," he said, shoving me into a stifling little room with a bare mattress on the floor. The room was full of eerie dark green light from the garbage bags taped over the window. "Neat effect, huh?" Bobby said. "Like Halloween, almost." I had never seen a window with an iron gate on the *inside*, but that's what there was. Bobby went over to it and tugged at the padlock. He didn't seem to care that he was grinding his grimy boots into the mattress. He punched the padlock a few times, as if his bicycle gloves were boxing gloves. "I told her the lock was fine," he said.

"You're a thorough person," I said.

Bobby brightened. "Now that's what I'm talking about," he said. "A little trust in my judgment."

I decided to push it a little further. "Sorry about back there in the van. You surprised me, that's all. I get that way when I'm upset. Plus I was just waking up."

"Well, that's okay," Bobby said. He was practically beaming. "I knew you couldn't be all the things Claire said. No one could." Then he wagged a finger at me, which made the glove straps flap a little. "Now you make sure to behave, young lady." Our relationship had clearly entered a new phase.

"I'm not looking for trouble," I said, which was actually true. The less attention they paid me, the better.

"You just rest now," said Bobby. "You're going to be out late tonight. Your Mom needs a little help with something."

But I wasn't out late that night. Or the next day, or the one after that.

chapter six

They kept me locked up in that coffin of a room for three days and three nights. At first, I thought I was just being punished. That would have been Mom's style. The fact that I saw only Bobby during that time was like her, too. She knew how to use your imagination against you.

Bobby brought me a pack of HoHos in the morning and maybe some chips at lunch and McDonalds or something for dinner. He told me we were "laying low." Meaning, I think, that the police were looking for me.

Lying there on the bare mattress those three days—Mom hadn't bothered with sheets, she thought they just made for a lot of extra work—I had plenty of time to think about my predicament. I'm not big on wallowing, but I felt that my life had taken a giant step backward. My grandparents were jerks to Silvia, and they had lots of annoying rules, but at least they tried to be nice. Mom, on the other hand, lived without rules, which was both good and bad, but mostly bad. The lack of rules occasionally worked to my advantage. For instance, the lobster night. We were living in Maine then, in a cabin. Mom and her boyfriend had gone out in a rowboat in the middle of the night and stolen a bunch of lobsters from lobstermen's pots. They waited until the lobsters were cooked before waking me up, so when they carried me to the picnic table, there was a big plate of steaming lobsters and some melted butter, and my Mom put a bib on me, which made me feel taken care of. I still remember her breath on my cheek, and the little kiss she gave me, which smelled like white wine and perfume.

That time was nice. There was also a time when she would wake me up almost every night—she didn't have a boyfriend then—and take me for long drives. I would be cranky for a while on account of being woken up, but pretty soon I'd roll down my window—it always seemed to be summertime when I was with her—and let the night air blow my hair around. Mom would find some bad country music on the radio and we would just drive and drive *wherever*, no destination, always winding up somewhere interesting, though, like a truck stop full of men who missed their kids and were extra nice to me. Or the ocean, where she'd drive us right down one of those private little streets, the ones beyond the boardwalk, where only rich people are allowed. Mom would pull the car right up to the end of the street, which would be covered in sand. We'd open the doors and listen to the ocean. I always wanted to go in the water, but Mom was afraid of it. She said that the ocean at night was the most frightening place she could imagine. Hearing her say that only made me want to go in more. I wasn't the least bit afraid. To me, the night ocean was amazing. Even back then, the idea of a place where Mom couldn't go appealed to me.

Mornings after those long drives I'd be too tired to go to school, not that I really wanted to. Mom would let me sleep in. Sometimes, if she was feeling especially guilty about taking me driving, she'd make me breakfast, complete with a big dessert. She didn't believe in nutrition, which she said was invented by greedy vegetable farmers.

Those were nice times, but Mom could also be wild in a bad way, especially when she was in one of her funks. Her funks could last a long time. The worst one I remember lasted almost two months. She barely got out of bed at all. I almost called the police, because the things she was saying scared me. She was crying a lot and she always seemed to be saying goodbye. She came out of it, though, like always. She'd wake up one day and suddenly everything was okay. That's when she'd go get a new boyfriend, or put up curtains, or have the rugs cleaned. She was very keen on fresh starts.

The way she would suddenly be in a funk, and then just as suddenly be out of one, took a toll on me. I never knew what to expect, and I guess I got into a funk of my own, because for a long time I wouldn't eat, or, if Mom made me, I'd eat the absolute minimum, and even that was hard to keep down. Mom thought I was doing it on purpose. She said I was just trying to get attention, but I wasn't. Food just stopped appealing to me. I had a metallic taste in my mouth all the time. I finally got her to stop trying to force feed me. She said she guessed I'd eat when I was good and ready, and hoped that would happen before I starved to death. Honestly, at the time, I think I would have been happy to starve. I remember not caring at all, about anything.

I must have looked pretty bad—I'd been avoiding mirrors for a while—because one day when Mom was out, my grandparents stopped by to see me, and my grandmother burst into tears when I opened the door. Mom's place was filthy, as usual. My grandmother kept telling me everything was going to be okay. My grandfather was clenching his jaw, the way he does when he's super angry. He said, "Let's get the girl out of this hellhole." Later, he told me they'd been watching the apartment building for almost two days, waiting until it looked as though my mother'd be gone for a while.

That's when I started living with my grandparents. They brought me in front of a judge, who agreed that they should take care of me. He was a friendly judge, not intimidating at all, the way you'd expect someone to be who decides people's fates every day. He asked me if I wanted to live with my grandparents.

"I suppose," I said. "If it's not too much trouble." That made the judge laugh, and he granted them custody of me, and then he issued something called a "restraining order," which was supposed to keep my Mom away from me. Obviously, restraining orders don't always work.

I thought about all of this, and then I thought about my Dad, which I almost never do when I'm angry because it makes me cry and then I get angry at him, too, or at least the memory of him, for making me cry. In a way, I was glad that my Mom didn't keep any mementos of him around, because I don't think I could have gotten through those three days if there had been.

* * *
* *

chapter seven

What Mom "needed help with," it turns out, was robbing my grandparents.

"Those two are loaded," she said. "They're worse than Jews. They've probably got money sewn into every mattress in the house." There was no point in telling Mom she was being idiotic. She wouldn't have listened. Besides, it was nice just to let her go on being wrong.

My grandparents are paranoid about cash. They're always running out and getting twenty or thirty dollars from the bank. There's never much more than that in the house, except when they go out of town. When they do go on a trip, they like to leave a hundred dollars on the table in the front hallway as they're locking up, along with a note to any thief—Dear Intruder!—saying to please take the money and not make a mess ransacking the house. Personally, if I were a thief, I'd take the money and then I'd ransack the house for more, but I guess that means I think like a thief, whereas they think like grandparents.

On the third night, Mom, Bobby, and I took the van over to my grandparents' house to "scope things out." I had been cooped up for so long that I didn't even mind what we were doing. It was enough just to be outside, breathing outside air, and to see the sky, even if it was the dishwatery city sky, with its pale orange haze. On the way across town, Mom asked me a lot of questions about my grandparents, mainly having to do with their habits. It was a Thursday—at least that's what Mom told me. It's amazing how quickly you can forget the day of the week—and even though it wasn't true, I said that my grandparents always stayed in on Thursdays and watched their boring antiques show. Mom said that it didn't matter because we weren't going "inside" tonight anyway. She said that I better not be lying about the antiques show, because if we got there and there was no sign of the TV being on, she'd cut my hair.

This was more of a punishment than it sounds. She had done it once before when she was angry. She used pinking shears, those huge fabric scissors with triangle teeth. The scissors were dull and rusty, and she wound up tearing out almost as much hair as she cut. The hair that was left looked like it had been chewed off by a dog. The next day, when she saw what she had done and how much it embarrassed me, she was very apologetic, but I guess she didn't really mean her apology, because here she was, threatening to do it all over again.

I said that we wouldn't be able to tell if they were watching TV, because the TV was in a room that had no windows. Besides, I said, the point wasn't that they watched the TV show. It's that they made a whole evening of it, with popcorn, et cetera.

"See?" Bobby said, clucking the van's horn. "She's very observant. She's a natural for this line of work." Mom told him to shut up, which he did, but not before complaining about how Mom was undermining his authority.

The van, which was corroded and had huge tires and the bikini barbarians on the side, didn't exactly fit into my grandparents' neighborhood. Mom knew it, too. She told Bobby to keep the van moving, and when we did stop, she was constantly telling him to avoid the streetlights. There are streetlights everywhere in my grandparents' neighborhood, which used to annoy me on nights when I couldn't sleep. Now, I was grateful for them.

We parked across from their house and a few cars down. I hoped to catch a glimpse of my grandmother or grandfather, but no luck. It was probably just as well. The sight of one of them padding around in a wool bathrobe would have made me too lonely.

A police cruiser glided down the street toward us. Its lights weren't flashing, but Bobby said, "That's our cue to skee-daddle." Mom told him to please shut his cakehole. Then she softened and said it was probably just a routine visit, on account of the kidnapping. It surprised me to hear her use the word "kidnapping." I hadn't thought of it that way since the first night.

At any rate, Mom turned out to be right. The policeman parked right across from us. The whole time he was getting out of his car, Bobby was freaking. Mom said, "I swear to God, if you don't shut up…" Then she turned her threats on me. "You make one sound…" she said.

The policeman didn't notice us. He walked slowly up to my grandparents' door, flipping pages on his clipboard, as if he was about to take an exam. He straightened his hat before he knocked on the front door. I kept thinking of those rusty scissors. I whispered, "Please, please, please be home." Then the light went on in the hallway.

At that point, Mom let Bobby drive us away. He kept trying to explain himself, saying how the policeman wouldn't have bothered him if he was scoping out the place solo. "I was thinking of you two, not me," he said, but Mom said that that was a load of bull, and for once, I agreed with her. Nobody said anything more until we were on the freeway.

Mom perked up at highway speed. She said she was hungry and asked Bobby to take her to the Krispy Kreme. Mom's not a big donut eater, so I figured she was making a peace offering. Bobby stomped on the gas and said, "Yes, Ma'am!"

★*★

Sometimes stereotypes are helpful, which makes me wonder why people are always telling you to avoid them. Marian says that stereotypes Trample the Inalienable Rights of the Individual, or something like that, but I say: why *not* use them, if they're almost always true? The stereotype I'm thinking of here is a fairly minor one: the fact that there's always a police car parked in front of a donut shop. People like to make jokes about policemen and donuts, probably because they're afraid of the police and like to imagine them as big donut-eaters. There's definitely something childish about eating donuts. It's hard to imagine someone being violent if you can picture him stuffing his face with a French cruller.

Lock me up for Trampling the Inalienable Rights, but there was a shiny police cruiser parked sloppily in the handicapped space in front of the Krispy Kreme. One cop was in the cruiser, fiddling with the radio. The other cop was ordering donuts at the counter. The bright lights and colors and the spotless glass walls made the insides of the Krispy Kreme look like a game show.

Bobby said something lame about criminals and cops not being so different because they both liked Krispy Kremes. When I said that we weren't criminals because we hadn't broken any laws yet, he said, "Speak for yourself," in an extremely pompous way. Mom laughed in his face and said that where she grew up, B.O. wasn't a federal offense. Bobby tried to look hurt by that comment, but he was clearly excited by the prospect of donuts.

It was hard to imagine why Bobby would marry a woman who was so mean to him, but I was learning that some people actually liked that. And besides, Mom was a very beautiful woman, in a wild kind of way, when she wanted to be. She never had a problem attracting men. Since Dad, she'd just been specializing in losers.

I asked if I could run to the bathroom. Mom didn't want to let me. She told me I could hold it until we got back, but I pointed out that there was a pretty long line in the Krispy Kreme and that "casing my grandparents' house"—which was what Bobby insisted on calling it— had been a little scary, which made me have to pee even more. Mom finally agreed, but not without threatening to come in with me. I knew that what she really wanted was to wait in the van and have a cigarette, so I said, "Fine, be my guest." She gave me a hard look, but finally told me to go on and hurry up. I thanked her, if you can believe it. I really did have to pee and it would have been nothing for her to say "too bad" and make me hold it until we got back to her place.

Bobby was at the counter, involving all the customers in helping him choose his donuts. He was in hog heaven, probably because he's so rarely the center of attention. He grinned when he saw me, flexing his thick continuous monobrow, as if to say, "Is this place not the greatest?" I ignored him and went to the ladies room.

On my way out of the Krispy Kreme, I bumped into the policeman, who was packing up his coffee and donuts at the counter by the door. I apologized. He gave me a very friendly policeman wink, which carries a lot more meaning than the average wink, at least in my book, because the person doing it is wearing a gun.

Seeing the policeman up close reminded me of Dad for some reason. Dad was definitely the kind of person who would wink at you if you bumped into him. It wasn't just the wink. There was something else. Maybe it was the barbershop powder smell. A lot of policemen smell like barbershop powder. Dad did, too.

Bobby came up behind me and handed me a box of donuts and

put his fat fingers around my arm. I don't know why, but in front of that policeman, Bobby's hand on me made me feel guilty, as if I actually *had* broken into my grandparents' that night, and not just scoped it out. I wasn't worried. I knew I could fool the policeman into thinking I was perfectly innocent.

A school counselor told me once that lying can be a kind of survival skill, like knowing how to drink water from a cactus or eat raw frogs. I could see that, but it still didn't make it right.

Bobby was shoving me along, saying, "Your Momma's waiting, tiger," as if he was my real Dad. I caught myself automatically starting to pretend that I was his daughter. Suddenly, I caught a glimpse of the life in store for me with Mom and Bobby—a night-time, liar's life, without rules. Instead of just being pushed towards the door, it was as if I was being pushed out to sea. The confusing part was that I loved the sea, only not enough to want to drown in it.

Bobby squeezed my arm again, right on one of the fence scratches. Without even thinking about it, I stopped in front of the policeman and said, "This man is kidnapping me."

The policeman looked around at the other people in the Krispy Kreme to see if they were laughing, which they weren't, but then he started laughing. Everyone else joined in, even Bobby. "Kidnapped, huh?" said the policeman, more to the people at the counter than to me. "Then maybe you should call the police." Everybody thought that was hilarious. The policeman elbowed Bobby in the ribs and said, "Cute kid." Bobby grinned and said, "She's a pistol." Then Bobby herded me out of the store. I didn't bother to say anything else to the policeman. It would have been pointless.

Outside the Krispy Kreme, Bobby told me that what I had just done was super dumb, but I knew he wasn't going to rat me out. He was mad, but ratting me out would have gotten him in worse trouble than me.

I thought things were okay when I climbed into the van, but Mom was waiting for me in the back of the van. She had seen everything, or at least enough, because after we pulled out of the Krispy Kreme lot and were safely on the highway, she came over and hit me in the face with her fist.

It got me partly in the eye, but mostly on my nose, which tends to bleed easily. "What was that for?" I said, hunching over to avoid ruining my clothes. I was not going to cry in front of her.

Of course I knew why she had hit me, and she knew that I knew. She didn't bother to explain. Instead, she went over and opened the side door, which you're never supposed to do when the van is moving, and definitely not at highway speed. The wind roared into the van and rocked it back and forth. Hamburger wrappers and drink lids swirled into the air, which was suddenly full of white dust. Bobby hit the brakes and said, "What the hell?" Mom turned to me and shouted, "You want out?"

The car in the lane next to us swerved and honked. Mom leaned out the open door, gave the driver the finger, and started screaming that he should mind his own business. Bobby was shouting back over his shoulder, asking Mom to please get back inside the van. She stayed out there for a second, facing the wind, chin up, her eyes shut. Her gorgeous hair whipped her shoulders. Then she stared down at the wet pavement for a while. She was crouching by the open door like a troll guarding a magic gate. She flung her arm out into the sixty-mile-an-hour wind, which made her hand fly up like a bird. She turned to me and said, "You want out? Go ahead. Be my guest."

The dark trees and the concrete walls of the highway streamed behind her in bars of angry color while she waited for my answer. I didn't give her one. Then she slid the door shut, forcing it against the wind, which was no match for her powerful arms and legs.

After that, everything seemed silent except the windshield wipers, which squeaked against the windshield. Apparently, it had started to rain. Bobby offered me a donut after a while. I wanted to eat one—I hadn't really eaten all day—but I was afraid of what Mom would do if I did, so I said I wasn't hungry. Bobby offered to save me one for later, but Mom told him not to bother.

She said I'd had enough for one night.

chapter eight

I managed to stall Mom and Bobby for a few more days by making up things about my grandparents' habits, but I didn't count on my Mom remembering that Monday was the anniversary of my Dad's death, the day my grandparents always drove to the cemetery to visit his grave. The grave was in an old family plot, a couple of hours away by car. Friends of theirs lived near the cemetery. After visiting the grave, there was always a little party with drinks in my Dad's memory. It was the only day of the year when both of my grandparents drank cocktails. They spent the night at their friends' house, so neither one would have to drive.

I've never been to see the grave myself. I was too scared to go when it all happened, and since then, I've had some other chances but I always turned them down. It's just not how I want to remember him.

I couldn't very well tell Mom that my grandparents had stopped visiting their son's grave. Mom wouldn't have believed me, because she knew better than anyone how devoted my grandparents were to Dad. I doubt I could have lied about it anyway, since it's such an emotional topic for me.

So Mom, Bobby, and I found ourselves parked outside my grandparents' house again on Monday night, only this time there wasn't a police car sitting out front. What's more, all the streetlights on their block were out, which Bobby and I both took as a sign of luck, only opposite kinds.

"Here's how it's going to work," Mom said. "You're going to take Bobby in with you. You're going to turn off the alarm, and then you're going to show him where the good stuff is."

"What good stuff?" I said.

Mom told me there'd better be some good stuff. "If I think you're holding out on us," she said, "I'm going to go in there myself, and God help that house. You better pray your grandparents aren't home when I come back and burn it to the ground."

Coming from anyone else, I wouldn't have worried about the last part. Lots of people talk about hurting other people, especially when they're angry, but most of the time it's just talk. I knew that in her right mind Mom would never hurt my grandparents, not because she felt sentimental about them, which she didn't, but because of the huge consequences if she got caught. But she was capable of almost anything when she was in one of her funks. I hadn't seen any evidence of a funk, but that didn't mean one wasn't just around the corner.

I finally told her about a few things that sounded pretty valuable, leaving out the stuff that my grandparents actually cared about. Mom wrote down what she wanted. She slapped Bobby with her little notepad every once in a while to make sure he was listening.

As I was telling her about the silver and the crystal decanters and the china, an idea was beginning to form in my mind. It started with the feeling I had been having that my life was over. I had been cooped up in that airless bedroom for a whole week, except for the trip to scope out my grandparents' house and this one to actually rob them. I had had plenty of time to remember how bad things used to be with my mother and to look forward to more of the same. Bobby was making an effort to be decent to me, but an effort from Bobby was worse than no effort at all. One night, lying there on the sweaty mattress,

reading some teen magazine Bobby had bought for me, I had been surprised to hear a voice welling up inside me, suggesting very calmly that
I might be better off dead. After the initial weirdness, I found that
voice pretty persuasive.

Mom and Bobby were bickering. Mom wanted to steal everything
tonight. Bobby only wanted to steal things that my grandparents
wouldn't notice missing and come back for more some other night. His
laziness was truly in a class by itself. I closed my eyes and tried to con-
centrate on a good memory, the way I taught myself when Mom and
Dad were having one of their big fights. It didn't work very well. The
best I could do was reduce Mom and Bobby's bickering to a distant
buzzing. I couldn't block it out completely because it was a dangerous
buzzing, like the kind a wasp makes.

That's when I decided to kill myself.

Whenever I'm about to tell a very daring lie, a big one, which
could land me in a lot of trouble if it doesn't go over, I feel a kind of
pressure inside. My cheeks start to burn. All the branches of the lie
come into focus in my imagination—all the likely objections, what I'll
need to say in order to keep it going, and, finally, all the possible out-
comes. Marian tells me that cooking up a nice, complicated lie is a lot
like playing chess. She may be right about that. Personally, I've never
had much patience for games.

The key to this lie was figuring out how to be alone in the house.
When Mom and Bobby were done, and Bobby was making a big whiny
show of unbuckling his seat belt because he had lost the argument, I
said, "Bobby probably shouldn't come in with me."

Mom immediately tried to shut me up, but Bobby, who was still
wrestling with his seat belt because he so obviously didn't want to go
in the house, said, "Let's hear her out. This family's a team, right?"

Mom said that this was no time for any of my nonsense, but Bobby told me to go ahead. When I spoke, I spoke to him, because as good as I am at lying, I learned everything about the craft from my Mom. She's an expert. She can see through almost anything. For instance, I knew she'd notice the fact that I was talking to Bobby and not to her, and I even knew that she'd be suspicious of that fact alone, but I had no alternative. Looking at Mom while I was lying was not an option. It was like staring into the eyes of a snake.

"Bobby," I said, making it sound as much like "Daddy" as I could, "I'm not saying I don't *want* you to come along. It'd be easier if you did, because you could help carry things. Besides, being in a dark house gives me the creeps." I said that to make him feel good. Actually, being with Bobby was a million times creepier than being in a dark house. Bobby gave Mom an "I told you so" look. "I'd love it if you went with me," I said, "but I don't think it justifies the risk."

Bobby said, "What risk?" and Mom jumped in again and the two of them had a quick argument, which I took as a good sign. Mom told him that he was the worst thief she'd ever seen, and the dumbest, which hurt Bobby's feelings but only made him more stubborn. He waited until she was done and then he said that it never did any harm to listen.

"I understand why my Mom is worried," I said, "but the truth is, if I'm in the house alone, there's no crime. Technically speaking. Even though I'm with you now, that house is still technically where I live. So if I'm inside, and I get caught, the worst they can say is that I ran away and came back and tried to take some stuff from my grandparents. Not a big deal, right?" Bobby nodded and said, "I hear you."

"But if you're inside with me, and we get caught, that means that a criminal—a *real burglar*—namely, *you*—is in the house. Which means trouble, for sure."

Bobby thought about that and said, "She does have a point, Claire," which triggered another quick argument, this time about what a coward Bobby was, and couldn't he tell that I was up to something. If they let me inside the house, there was no telling what I'd do. Et cetera.

"I wouldn't want you to worry while I was in there," I said, "so I thought of a way around it. I'll take a watch into the house with me and I'll come out every three minutes with whatever I've found, even if I haven't found anything. Three minutes will be a kind of check-in time." Bobby was impressed with that. "Makes a lot of sense," he said, nodding.

"It doesn't take three minutes to call 9-1-1," Mom said.

"I thought of that, too," I said. "The phone in the front hallway is a portable. I'll bring that out first thing, and you can listen in and make sure I don't call anyone. If I tried it, you could hang up from the portable. You'd control the phone calls." Bobby was especially impressed with that. He called me a "real thinker." He meant it as a compliment, but he couldn't help sounding a little jealous.

"I don't like it," Mom said, but she couldn't say exactly why, and she couldn't deny that it was better if Bobby never had to go inside, especially if there were a lot of trips.

There was a third little argument, but it was the quickest, because Bobby knew that he didn't want to go in the house, and my Mom was wavering, and finally she ran out of nasty things to say to him, so it was decided.

chapter nine

Of course I had no intention of dying that night, at least not in the literal sense. I've always thought that killing yourself is a cowardly thing to do unless you're suffering from terminal cancer or something and you can't stand the pain. What I needed to do was to make Mom and Bobby *think* I was dead. That way, they wouldn't come looking for me.

Pretending to kill myself was not something I'd thought up completely on my own, although I wish I had. I got the idea from Marian, who'd been reading *The Adventures of Huckleberry Finn* and giving me a blow-by-blow every day at lunch. There's a part where Huck fakes his death so his crazy, murderous father won't follow him. I couldn't remember whether the plan worked in the book or not—it's impossible to listen to Marian day after day and not let your mind wander a little—but the part about faking a death seemed pretty sound.

I walked up to my grandparents' front door feeling like an imposter. I imagined that this was what a travelling salesman felt coming home after a long trip, forgetting for a minute that this was where he lived, and maybe practicing his phony little greeting as he approached the front door, wondering if the people inside were gullible and easy to rip off.

My key still worked. You'd think they would have changed the locks, but my grandmother can't stand workmen in the house. After I let myself in, it was sad to call out hello and get no answer. It was even sadder to be relieved that no one was home. Turning off the alarm wasn't the mindless ritual it used to be. Part of me was hoping that my grandparents had changed the numbers in the code, but it was still seven twenty-five, after July 25th, my birthday.

The first thing I did was to take the portable phone out to the van, just like I said I would. Mom snatched it from me and pressed the "Talk" button to make sure it worked. My grandparents kept the volume turned way up because my grandfather was going deaf. You could hear the dial tone from three feet away. Bobby said, "Good going, tiger!" and gave me his watch. He pointed to the clock in the dashboard and whispered, "Everything's synchronized." He wasn't even joking!

I was almost out the door when Mom kicked my butt—literally—which almost tripped me. "Three minutes," she said.

"I know, I promise," I said.

As soon as I was back inside, I went right to the kitchen and turned on the stove, all four burners, and the broiler, too. My grandmother never throws anything away, including kitchen appliances. She still has an ancient gas stove—the kind you have to light with a match. The gas was hissing loudly and already starting to stink when I closed the pocket door to the dining room. There was one other door to the kitchen, from the living room, which always stuck because it was warped. It took me a while to push it shut, and then I remembered the air conditioning vent under the kitchen table. I wasn't sure whether the vent was the kind that blew in air or sucked it out, so I went back in and closed it. It got a little claustrophobic under the kitchen table. The sound of the gas made the closed-up kitchen feel like it was inflating.

Next, I went right to my grandmother's jewelry box, which she keeps on her dresser, and picked out a few pieces that I knew she didn't like very much and which were mostly costume jewelry anyway.

I had prepared Mom in advance by saying that there wouldn't be too much good jewelry, since my grandmother kept the really nice stuff in a safety deposit box. That was actually true, and Mom knew it. She gave me an ironic look, and asked me what was the point of owning luxurious things if you kept them locked up in a vault your whole life. She said that people who locked things up like that didn't know how to live, and didn't deserve to have nice things. I didn't bother to tell her that people locked things up so they wouldn't lose them to moronic thieves like us.

According to Bobby's watch, I still had half a minute left, so I went to my grandfather's study and pulled a piece of stationery out of his desk. His drawers are full of giveaway pens because he's too cheap to buy them. By the time I found one that worked, I only had ten seconds to go, so I left the pen and paper by the door, ran out to the van, and handed Mom the jewelry.

"She's a regular cat burglar," Bobby said. Mom immediately started pawing the tangled chains. "This is a lot of junk," she said. "Pure junk." I kept quiet and waited for the top of the next minute. "Time for round two," I said. As I sprinted back to the house, I heard Bobby leaning back in the squeaky driver's seat and saying, "A guy could get seriously used to this." I could just picture the look on Mom's face.

Whatever I brought back this time had to be nicer than the jewelry. I went down to the basement and pulled out the wooden box where my grandmother kept her good silver. I brought it upstairs, left it by the door, and went to the kitchen to check on the gas. It was smelling pretty gassy, but I figured it still had a ways to go. Then I got the paper and pen, and in the remaining minute and a half, started a note to my grandparents. It basically said that I was sorry I had disappeared, but that it was Mom's fault, and that she had kept me locked up, which was why I hadn't called. Then I apologized for helping Mom and Bobby steal the jewelry and the silver. That's as far as I got before I had to run.

Bobby oohed and aahed over the silver, studying the salt dish and the ice tongs as if they had been made by an alien race, but Mom sensed something was up. "Three minutes, and that's all you got?" she said.

"It wasn't where she usually keeps it," I said. "I had to go digging in the basement."

"We don't have all night," Mom said, flicking Bobby's arm. "This time, you go in with her."

"I think she's doing great," he said, giving me a cheesy thumbs-up.

"This time I'm going for the crystal," I said. "It may take a little longer."

Mom gave me an icy look. "Three minutes," she said, and I knew she meant it. "There's no point taking it if it's all broken," Bobby said, but even he could see that his opinion was irrelevant. I was tempted to look back at my Mom as I ran back to the house. If my plan worked, I would never see her again. I almost did, but then I thought the better of it. It would have raised too many flags in her mind.

Once I was inside, I didn't waste any time with the crystal. I knew I wasn't going to make another trip out to the van. The kitchen was good and gassy, so I finished up my note to my grandparents. "Sorry for blowing up your kitchen," I wrote. "If it worked, I'll be explaining this in person. If not, thanks for everything you did for me. P.S. You were wrong about Silvia. She's a good person and she didn't deserve to be kicked out. P.P.S. If I'm dead when you read this, please bury me near Dad. Love, Chlo."

I signed it with some Xs and Os. I was crying a little, because thinking about where I wanted to be buried was serious, and writing the note made me remember the nice things my grandparents had done for me. Anyway, when I checked my watch, I only had thirty seconds left. That's when I remembered I needed matches. I opened the kitchen door, and tried to go in, but it was so full of gas that I started coughing right away and almost threw up. I pulled my shirt up over my nose and ran over to the stove, which is where my grandmother usually keeps her matches, but there were none there, so I had to go into the pantry closet to get a new box. By that time, I was five seconds over. I expected to hear the key in the door any second. Mom had made a copy so I wouldn't be able to lock them out of the house.

I made it out to the living room, but just barely. My head was pounding. The whole world smelled like gas. I said a word or two to Dad, to the effect that if I blew myself up for real, I hoped I'd see him soon. In some bizarre part of my mind, I found myself hoping my face wouldn't look too bad if it got burned. I pulled out a match and lit it. The living room didn't blow up, so I walked the tiny flame over to the kitchen, opened the door, and threw it in.

chapter ten

I learned something that night: it's almost impossible to keep a thrown match lit. It was out before it even left my fingers. The match fell to the floor, still glowing a little at the tip. The stove hissed away. I thought I heard faint laughter, but then I realized it was the crickets outside.

I was hoping that a glowing match tip might still be enough to ignite the gas, but then the tip died out and gave up a wisp of black smoke. I checked my watch. Half a minute late. Bobby's cowboy boots rang out on the front walk. His walk was very distinctive and irritating. He had a way of coming down hard on his heels and scraping them a little.

I needed some kindling, and fast. The best I could come up with was the apology note I had just written, which I had planned to leave on the table in the front hallway, next to the Intruder money.

My apology was the last thing I wanted to burn. I was afraid of what my grandparents would do with my body if they didn't have instructions, but I crumpled the note anyway and lit a corner. I held on until the whole sheet was burning. Then I tossed the burning note into the kitchen. It's odd, but thinking back, I can't imagine why I didn't feel the flames scorching my fingers.

That didn't work either! The blackened note curled and fluttered to the ground, devouring itself in glowing red rings. Bobby was at the front door. I could hear him fumbling with his keys, then dropping them. I even heard a faint "Oof" as he bent over to pick them up.

I had one last chance. I took a deep breath, held it, and dove into the kitchen for the big bag of charcoal my grandfather kept in the pantry closet. It was heavy, but I managed to drag it out. I pushed it nice and close to the oven, for good measure. I hadn't taken a breath. My muscles were shaking. I could barely keep my fingers still enough to light the match. The match didn't stay lit. I tried another one. It went out, too. In my imagination, the stove, fearing for its life, kept blowing them out. I finally got a corner of the bag lit. I had to blow on it to really get it going. I remember watching it take and admiring the purple and green flame. It reminded me how Dad and I used to throw the Sunday funnies in the fireplace when we had a fire going, just to see the ink flare up in strange colors. Don't ask me why I was so mesmerized. Blame it on the gas.

An explosion in real life isn't anything like what you see in the movies. Explosions in movies are almost always seen from the outside, or at least from a distance. They're beautiful. You usually get a big "whompf!" sound effect, and a slow-motion flameball. Slow motion is the opposite of what's it like in real life.

I did hear a sound, but it was a sort of negative sound, like a sound chasing itself backwards. Then there was unbelievable heat—like opening an oven, only times a thousand. That heat, I found out later, totally crisped my eyebrows and eyelashes. After the heat, I was still on the floor, but in the dining room, behind the table, lying on my left wrist funny, watching the polyester fringe on the curtains melt in drippy red corkscrews.

And that was it, at least all I remember of it. The windows were gone, and the front door, which Bobby was in the process of opening, had been blown shut by the explosion. There was the odd fire here and there in the carpeting, as if tiny pioneers had circled their wagons and were making camp for the night. Glowing charcoal briquettes had landed all over the place like meteors. The smoke detectors were screaming their heads off. I pulled myself up to the windowsill. Broken glass glistened in the shrubs and on the dewy lawn. The night air was thick and sweet.

Bobby was sitting on the front walk, rubbing his sore bottom and staring at the front door. He was probably wondering who had slammed it. He looked surprised and upset, somewhere between being pissed and wanting his Mommy.

The van was honking insistently. Bobby waved back over his shoulder to show that he was okay, but the van didn't seem interested in that. It kept honking. People were starting to come out their front doors. Bobby got up and brushed off his pants. His monobrow furrowed as he took in the broken windows. Instead of rushing into the house to save me, he squatted down and studiously poked at some broken glass. He wasn't more than ten feet away. It was stupid and careless of me to watch him. Bobby could have easily seen me, if he was an observant person. My head was right there, framed by the empty window. But I couldn't stop. It was like watching my own funeral. For all Bobby and Mom knew, I was dead. I pretended that the reason he couldn't see me was that I was a ghost.

The van was really honking now, if you can still call it honking when there's just one long blast of the horn. Bobby shook his head and put his hands on his hips. The only word he said was, "Damn," which, to me, sounded almost like an apology. Then he minced back over to the van. He was in a hurry, but he still managed to drag his heels a little.

Although I was glad he didn't actually do it—trust me!—I appreciated the fact that Bobby at least considered coming into the house after me, which is more than I can say for his wife. As the van pulled away, I tried to get one last look at her face, but she was hiding it with a magazine. Then the van turned the corner.

I lowered myself down to the carpet. It was hard to believe that they were really gone. I could still smell gas, but the outside air was coming in so it didn't smell very dangerous. I knew I should have been happy that my plan had worked, but I just sat there picking at bits of fused carpet and thinking that as low as my expectations were about some people, sometimes they weren't anywhere near low enough.

chapter eleven

T heoretically, I was dead. But that didn't mean I was safe.

The fire trucks were coming. There was no question about that. I didn't doubt that the firemen would be very nice when they arrived. A big gallant fireman with a mustache would probably offer me his heavy yellow jacket. I would have accepted it gladly, too, along with any snacks or juice he happened to foist on me.

The problem wasn't the fire department. It was the TV trucks. TV news people loved a good fire, particularly if there'd been an explosion. I knew for a fact that Mom and Bobby would be watching the news that night—Mom, to see close up what had happened; and Bobby, to prove to Mom how much danger he'd been in. They'd also be looking for pictures of me, their little thief, dead or alive.

I couldn't just ask the TV people not to show me. They'd do it anyway, no matter how good a reason I gave them. They love showing people who don't want to be seen, especially grieving families and victims of gunshots and fire. The less you want to be seen, the more the TV people want to show you. It's perverse, but true.

I would have loved to stay for the nice firemen, and then, in the morning, when my grandparents got back from visiting my father's grave, to apologize in person about destroying the house. But the TV people made that impossible. If Mom and Bobby saw me alive, they'd come get me. It was as simple as that.

I stood in the front hallway for a minute, even though I knew I had to go. I tried to force myself to think about the next step, but I kept getting distracted. It was strange to see what the explosion had blown up, and what it hadn't. For instance, I wouldn't have expected the curtains to drip the way they did, or the carpet to melt and pool in places like glass. I was just as surprised to see that the hundred dollars of Intruder money hadn't burned up, or even been ruffled. It was bizarre! A picture on the wall nearby was totally scorched, but the five twenties were still fanned out on the table in the hallway, just the way my grandmother had left them. So I took them. I figured that my grandparents would understand. They were always telling me not to leave the house without money.

I was too scared to scavenge any food or clean clothes. The gas was still on, and who knew how long it would be before the place blew up again?

It was time for phase two of my plan: the getaway. I ran down the basement stairs. The iron hand rail was still warm from the explosion, but everything else in the basement seemed normal. The door to the maid's apartment—Silvia's old room—was closed, as usual. My grandfather had a habit of closing it whenever he saw it open. The ping-pong table was stacked high with laundry. The bookcase shelves bowed under the weight of my grandparents' dusty encyclopedia. The car keys were in their usual place, a miniature fishbowl on one of the shelves. My grandparents had taken the fancy car, which meant I'd have the Dodge.

I took a long look back. The upstairs was crackling quietly and giving off a nasty smell. I know I should have felt sorry about blowing up the house—and I did—but I was still a little proud of myself. I thought, *Oh, well.* Then I opened the door to the garage.

The garage was pitch black, which was fine by me. I didn't want to turn on the light or open the garage door until the last second, in case there were any gawkers outside. The familiar smells of fertilizer and lawnmower and clean rubber tires made me feel oddly safe. I guided myself by touch, running my fingers along the garden hose that my grandfather had nailed to the garage wall to protect the car doors. Feeling my way along the wall, I had to smile. There was a time when the garage used to creep me out, when the sound of the motor and the grinding of the rusty wheels of the electric garage door opener would frighten me. That's how skittish I was when I first came to live with my grandparents.

I was fiddling with the car lock when I heard sobbing coming from the basement. I thought I'd been alone in the house the whole time. I hadn't counted on my grandparents getting another maid so soon.

It's embarrassing to say, but I almost didn't go back in the house. Call it my mother's stellar influence. I was scared. My body was beginning to hurt, my wrist in particular. I knew I had to get out of there. But the sobbing just went on and on. I wanted to scream, "Shut up!" but screaming was out of the question. Nobody in their right mind stays in a burning building and sobs—not even an ignorant Mexican.

Thinking of Silvia was what finally convinced me to go back in. I wasn't about to be responsible for someone's death. Honestly, if I hadn't thought of her, I might have just hit the road.

I knew I could walk right in to Silvia's old apartment. The door didn't lock. It was held shut by a magnet at the top. The knob didn't even turn. You just pulled it straight open, like a closet door. That had gotten me in trouble once or twice with Silvia and Roberto. I suppose there wasn't a real security reason to have a lock on it, but now, in light of what I knew about my grandparents, it made sense that they wouldn't want the maid to be able to lock her door.

Even before I opened the door and turned on the light, I knew who was inside. I could smell her.

It was Silvia. She wore a distinctive ultra sweet kiddie perfume, some berry or other—but she also used my grandfather's brand of deodorant. She said it reminded her of her father. So she gave off a confused smell, half man and half woman, which generally annoyed me. But for once, that mixed signal of hers was making me incredibly happy.

Silvia's sobbing was so scary and intense, for a moment I thought she might be having her baby. I turned on the light. There she was, sitting on the floor with her skinny little legs splayed out in front of her, her round belly resting like a basketball on her lap. She aimed a hammered tin cross at me and started screaming in Spanish. She seemed to think I was some kind of demon.

It took a minute or two to calm her down enough to talk. I kept saying, "It's just Chlo, it's Chlo." She waved her finger at me each time I said it, as if saying my own name was a no-no. "If you're who you say you are," she said, "then stand over there." Meaning, in front of the mirror, to prove I had a reflection. She was being absurd, but I understood a little better when I saw myself in the mirror. My chin was smudged black from the windowsill. That plus the missing eyebrows and eyelashes did make me look pretty ghoulish, not to mention the fact that the left side of my hair was all curled up from the heat, which made it look like I had gotten a lunatic perm, or at least half of one.

Silvia made me take a test to prove that I was really me. She asked a bunch of questions, things that only I would have known, such as, What was her favorite kind of pizza? I answered, "Ham and pineapple." What was her favorite movie? "Gone with the Wind."

"See?" I said. Silvia grimaced.

"That doesn't prove anything!" she said.

I told her it wasn't my fault if she asked bad questions.

"You confused me," she said. "It wasn't fair."

"How?" I said. *"How?"*

"You've got ways."

"All right," I said. "One more question."

Silvia had already thought up the ultimate puzzler. "What was the name of the first teddy bear Roberto gave me?"

"That's a trick question!" I said. "He gave you about ten, all at the same time."

"Then the first big one."

"Fuzzy or hairy?"

"Fuzzy."

"Tito P.," I said. "After some dumb musician."

Silvia started sobbing again. "Oh, Chica," she said. "It *is* you. Thank God." She reached up and pinched my cheeks, which stung like they were sunburnt. Then she pulled me down next to her and kissed my lips and said, "Sweetie, we thought you were dead!"

From what I could gather between blubbery hugs—which were still punctuated now and then by sudden piercing looks, just in case I really was a demon—Silvia was overdue to have her baby. "The baby won't come and the doctors tell me nothing, but then I figured it out—God is unhappy with me. I'm so unfortunate! I left my saints." She opened a paper bag and showed me what was inside: two picture frames made out of flattened coffee cans, with tacky religious scenes in them; some fat candles with printed hocus pocus that's supposed to come true as the candle burns; some bits of metal in the shapes of human body parts, that she said were for praying. And of course the tin cross, which she still wouldn't let me touch and which she kept more or less pointed in my direction. For insurance, I suppose.

Silvia had somehow gotten it into her head that God was punishing her for leaving all that stuff behind. That's the kind of thing I hate most about religion, that it takes perfectly good people with real problems and gives them the worst kind of nonsense to worry about.

I personally didn't agree with her convictions, but I didn't argue with her—she was still very freaked. She thought that the explosion upstairs was the Devil come to destroy her. "And you, Chica, are my angel, sent from God as a sign that coming back here was the right thing." I thanked her for that, because thinking someone is an angel is pretty nice, even if it is a load of baloney.

I told her we had to get out of the house because it was still on fire. "Whatever you say, anything. Really," Silvia said, brushing my shoulders. I was a mess, there's no denying it, but she was treating me like a Hollywood celebrity or something, so I told her to please cut it out.

Silvia objected to taking the Dodge. She never called it "stealing," exactly, but that was clearly what she was thinking. I told her we had to take it. I asked her if she wanted me to be kidnapped again. It was a low blow, but we had wasted too much time already playing twenty questions. "Oh, no," she said. "In that case, the car is necessary."

This was *my* escape, *my* plan, and I wasn't about to let Silvia drive, but I banged my wrist against the steering wheel as I was climbing into the Dodge. The pain was so harsh I had to twist my legs out of the car and put my head down between them to keep from throwing up. I had never seen a bruise like the one that was coming in—it was all yellow-green and nasty. Now there was no question about my driving. Even I knew better than to try it one-handed.

I wasn't sure Silvia could fit behind the wheel, on account of her enormous belly, but together we managed to push the seat back. Just as we figured out how to tilt the steering wheel up and out of the way, we heard the first fire truck pulling up around front. Its idling engine made the hanging garden tools rattle against the wall of the garage.

The Dodge started up fine, but instead of getting going, Silvia sat there with her head bowed. "Can we please just go?" I said. Silvia said she wasn't going anywhere without saying a prayer first, and that I had to say it with her. She could be extremely stubborn. I helped her say her stupid prayer. At least I let her glom onto my good hand while she said something very fervent in Spanish. She looked up at me with her big gooey eyes when she finished and squeezed my hand until I said "Amen." I was annoyed with her for holding me hostage to a prayer like that. People shouldn't do that to one another. It's bad manners.

Then there was nothing holding us back. I got the garage door going. Silvia wasn't quite used to the new distance to the pedals. When she released the emergency brake, the Dodge gunned forward. We shot out of the garage and down the driveway, narrowly missing a fireman who had made his way around the house. I waved to him as we lurched around the corner. I meant it as an apology. The fireman waved back with his yellow-handled ax. He didn't seem too angry, but then, I might have been reading into it. He mouthed the words, "Take it easy," like a teacher whose students are crazy for recess.

chapter twelve

o! Go! Go! was all I could think as we left the house behind. My stomach muscles were all tensed up from wanting to go faster. It didn't feel much like freedom, at least not at first. I ducked down at the first sign of anything remotely resembling a van. After a while, though, Silvia's constant chatter about Roberto, and the familiar insides of the Dodge—the creaky vinyl, the smell of cherry cough drops—all went to work on me and I began to relax. I stared out the window while Silvia drove. She took us up on the freeway. The road hummed reassuringly. The highway lights smiled down on us. Everything started to fall away: the explosion, my mother, the whole sleeping city, with its empty factories and broken down houses.

I was feeling a strange mix of lightness and heaviness, as if I had just hauled myself up onto a sun-baked raft after a long night treading water. It was a while before I even asked Silvia where we were going. She said "California," as if crossing the country was the easiest thing in the world. In my frazzled mind, California seemed as good as any place. I had a hundred dollars in my pocket. We had a full tank of gas. I asked Silvia if she knew how to get there. She said something about God pointing the way. At the time, even that kind of thinking didn't annoy me too much.

I dozed with my head rattling against the window, but it was the worst kind of sleep, where something really hurts and you wake up every two minutes because of the pain. I had seen a teething baby cry in its sleep. I suppose that's what I was like. When the pain in my wrist wasn't jarring me, it was Silvia, gently shaking my thigh and saying, "It's just a nightmare. There's no need to cry, Chica."

Then I must have finally fallen into a deeper sleep, because I opened my eyes to the morning sun in the side view mirror. Silvia's window was half open, which made it very loud inside the car, but I didn't mind. The wind chafed my face, but I loved all that air anyway. I asked if we were in California yet. I meant it as a joke, because California is days and days away by car, but Silvia apologized for the trip taking so long. She said she thought we might be getting close.

At that point, I started to pay attention to the road. There was something familiar about it, but then there's always something familiar about highways. They're all pretty much the same, at least the big ones, except for the signs. We were in a stretch where the signs weren't particularly helpful, but occasionally we spotted one that told us we were going west. I figured we couldn't be doing all that badly. California was nothing if not west.

But then, after about twenty minutes, the sign changed and told us we were going south, which was strange because we hadn't taken any exits. The traffic started to get heavy, which was also suspicious. After crawling along for ages, we came to another sign. This one said we were going east. Then I recognized one of the exits from when my grandparents used to take me over to see one of their friends who lived on the other side of town. "We're on the Beltway!" I shouted.

The needle on the gas gauge said, "Empty." Silvia had been circling the city all night. I tried to explain what had happened, but Silvia refused to understand. In her mind, we were halfway to California. "I didn't make a turn," she said, shaking her head confidently, "never once." She at least agreed that we needed gas, so we pulled off at the next exit.

I was sure Silvia was hungry, even if she was too sheepish to admit it just then, so I suggested that we stop at a Taco Palace. I felt guilty about getting so mad at her. It wasn't her fault that she didn't know how to navigate. The roads are more complicated in America than in Mexico. That's why we use maps here.

Silvia pooh-poohed the Taco Palace. She said that the food there wasn't what Mexicans really ate, but what Americans *thought* Mexicans ate, which, in her mind, painted an ugly picture of Americans. I didn't want to get into a fight with her, although I liked the food at Taco Palace. I thought it was pretty ungrateful of her to reject it as not Mexican enough.

We finally stopped at a hamburger place, but Silvia didn't approve of that, either. When it came to ordering, she just got some orange juice and toast. She threw most of it out. I told her she had to eat, for the baby, but she claimed she wasn't very hungry and that she'd eat tons when we got to California. She said that Roberto was a great cook. As for me, I wished that it was lunchtime, because what I really wanted was a hamburger, or maybe even two, but it was still early in the morning, and all they were serving was breakfast. It's funny how you can be hungry for the wrong meal. My appetite clock had gotten pretty messed up at my mother's house.

After breakfast, we gassed up the car. Silvia spent a lot of time in the Mini-Mart at the gas station. She came out with some surprisingly nice fruit, some cookies, and a bottle of lemon-lime fizzy water, which is my favorite. She also had a carton of milk, which she opened before we got back in the car. She asked me to hold it and give her sips as we drove.

When we were back on the Beltway, Silvia said that the sooner we got to California, the better, so we should keep driving as long as we could, not even stopping to pee, if we could help it. I knew that not stopping to pee would be a big personal sacrifice for her, because her bladder was so tiny on account of the baby.

I was making a big sacrifice, too, but I didn't mention it. My wrist was so swollen I could barely move it. I had borrowed some scotch tape from the gas station attendant to wrap my fingers together and keep them still. Moving them—even the slightest jiggle—caused the worst pain, even worse than the time my jaw was broken and nobody found out about it for almost a week.

I was playing with the bendy straw in Silvia's milk carton, trying to straighten it out, because when it was bent back, it reminded me of my wrist. Silvia asked for a sip. I held the carton up to her. There was a fuzzy picture of a lost kid printed on the side, under the words "HAVE YOU SEEN THIS GIRL?"

It was a picture of me!

I never paid much attention to the missing children ads on milk cartons. The faces didn't look real to me. And then there was the problem of not knowing the story behind the ad. What if the kid had run away for a good reason, like a live-in uncle who kept trying to climb into her bed, or a father who spent too much time sitting at a table with a gun and a bottle of whiskey? I had heard that sometimes they used computers to age the children in the pictures, and that idea bothered me, too. It was as if you were never allowed to get away. You'd be running all your life, or at least the years until you were 21, which is the most important part of a life, anyway.

Silvia got all excited about my being on the milk carton. "Hey, you're famous!" she said, but that was the whole problem. Luckily, they had chosen an awful picture, the one they took on my first day at Field. The photographer had literally forced me to smile. I hadn't wanted to.

I hated being photographed. It always made me feel like a criminal. Back then, I was especially sensitive, which made me lash out. I asked the photographer why he didn't have a *real* job. He said he had nothing better to do than wait all day for me to smile. So I said I had nothing better to do all day than make him lose a lot of money for being an idiot. That got him. I could tell from his ratty shirt that he needed the money. He walked over to me, put his fingers on the corners of my mouth, and pushed upwards. "Smile," he said. "Like *this*." The fact that he touched me was pretty shocking. His assistant took the picture before I had time to react. So I did have a smile in the picture—at least an ironic one—but the rest of my face was extremely pissed.

There was a description of me under the picture. Most of it was right, but they listed my eye color as "hazel," which was a surprise because I had always thought of them as plain brown. "Hazel" had to have been my grandmother's touch. I could just picture her talking to the HAVE YOU SEEN THIS GIRL? people over the phone and pausing for a minute when they asked what my eye color was, thinking that I might read the milk carton someday, and wanting to help with my "positive self-image," so telling them that my eyes were "hazel," which was a real stretch. My grandfather would be hovering around while she placed the call, playing out the telephone cord so she wouldn't get tangled in it, because she tended to pace when she was making a difficult call, and then, when she was finally a little calmer and sitting down at the kitchen table, standing behind her and rubbing her neck with his papery hands.

I was tempted to call the 800 number on the carton and let them know I was okay, but I decided not to. Who knew what kind of wiretap they'd have on the phone? The mission now was to get Silvia to California to have her baby. I'd gotten her kicked out and almost blown up. I wasn't about to get her deported.

Part of me didn't mind the idea of my grandparents worrying a little, either. Frankly, I felt like I was cleaning up their mess.

By now, Silvia was yawning almost constantly. She needed to rest. I knew she wouldn't stop on her own, so I told her I was sorry but I was still really tired. I asked if we could go to her place to rest up a bit, since we were still in town. "It's not too far, that place," she said. She added that we'd never get to California at this rate, but I could tell she liked the idea of stopping.

We went part of the way around the Beltway again until we hit a stretch Silvia recognized. She never did own up to the night of driving in circles, but it was such a gorgeous day, who cared? Being on the road was relaxing. I turned on the radio and tried to find something good, but after I while I left it alone. Everything I heard sounded fine.

We got off the Beltway at a new exit. The usual fast food places were being built, but no malls yet. The road was wide and very smooth. It was so new it didn't even have lines painted on it. You could tell from the old wooden fences and the flat fields with a single enormous tree in the middle that this used to be farm country. Instead of cows by the side of the road, there were billboards with paintings of fancy houses and the words "Coming Soon!" Bright orange surveyor's flags fluttered like poisonous butterflies in the fields. Bulldozers were busy tearing up the land. I saw a group of men pulling down a grain silo with ropes. They looked so old-fashioned, silhouetted against the sun—like pioneers, only instead of building the country, they were tearing it down. I wondered why they weren't using machines.

Then, suddenly, the wide road ended, narrowing into its old, patched, humble self. Up ahead, there was still farmland, but you could tell it was doomed. Silvia pulled into the parking lot of a brand new hotel. Its sign wasn't even installed yet. It lay on the ground under a blue tarp. When the tarp caught the breeze, I made out the words "Alamo Inn." Americans were always telling everyone to remember the Alamo. I hoped Silvia wasn't too sensitive about the name. After all, it referred to a huge defeat for her people—at least I thought it did.

There were flowers in wooden planters in the parking lot. The woodwork was all freshly painted. There was an ornamental pond with a few underfed carp cowering in the shadow of lilies. "Wait here," Silvia said. Then she waddled off, following an extension cord up a set of exterior stairs to the balcony along the second floor. She climbed slowly, leaning heavily on the rail every few steps to catch her breath. I felt like warning her about wet paint. At one point, she turned back to me and waved, which let me see her in profile. She was so huge!

After a few minutes, Silvia waved me upstairs, where she introduced me to her friend, a maid named Rosaria. Rosaria said to call her "Rosie." Rosie was a mousy little thing with a pock-marked chin and a lipful of hair. She used her master key to let us into one of the rooms. "It's yours till six," she said. Silvia kissed Rosie's greasy cheeks and whispered something in her ear that made her blush.

We sat in soft upholstered chairs while Rosaria gave the room a quick once-over with her vacuum and made the bed. It's hard to imagine a feeling more luxurious than watching someone make up a bed for you with nice starchy sheets. It was like being an aristocrat.

I asked Silvia if we should tip Rosaria. She said, "Come on!" as if I had just insulted her, which I guess I had. In my defense, I wouldn't expect one of my friends, whose job it was to clean rooms every day, to clean one just for me, especially if she was going to have to do it again in a few hours. I told Silvia she had a nice friend in Rosaria. She didn't say anything, but I could tell she agreed.

As soon as Rosaria left, Silvia and I flopped on the bed and turned on the TV. The hotel had cable. There wasn't much on, but we didn't care. We had a remote. Flipping through the channels was like reading a fat Chinese menu, the kind that's as thick as a magazine. A lot of the dishes may sound downright disgusting, but the main point is the possibility of ordering them.

I like hotel rooms nice and cold, so I turned down the temperature. Silvia complained, but I wrapped her up in a blanket and she was fine.

There was a phone in the bathroom, right next to the toilet. "Check it out!" I said. Silvia nodded. "It's a luxurious place," she said. I liked the way Silvia pronounced "luxurious." I made her say it again. I unwrapped one of the plastic cups on the sink and filled it up with tap water, which wasn't half bad. I brushed my knuckles against one of the towels while I drank. "The towels are nice and soft," I said approvingly, as if I was considering buying them.

A few minutes later, lying on the slightly scratchy bedcover, knowing that I could peel it back and slip between the cool sheets with Silvia, and her all excited because we were on our way to California—it was as close to happy as I had been in a long time. "Hey—why don't you give Roberto a call?" I said.

"No telephoning," Silvia said. "Rosaria said, 'No.'"

"Just one call?" I said. "You know you want to."

"Of course I want to," she said, "but I'm not." The thought of calling Roberto seemed to make Silvia sad, so I offered to run her a bath. She said no thanks, because it was too hard to get in and out of the tub, but she told me to go ahead. She said she thought I could really use one.

Looking in the bathroom mirror, I had to agree with her. I ran a steaming bath. There were lots of little bottles of complimentary hotel goo. I poured it all in. The water got bubbly and smelled like almonds, and changed color to bright blue, like the Caribbean. I tested it with my big toe, and when I was sure I hadn't created an acid bath that would eat off my flesh, I lowered the rest of me under that exotic water, even my head. That was a mistake, because my cheeks still felt sunburned, and hot water was the last thing they needed. Once I got over that, it was just me and the nice almondy bubbles.

Even my wrist stopped bothering me after a while, which meant that I could focus on other things, like the sound of the bathroom fan, which had turned on automatically when I switched on the light. It made a high drone like a bumblebee, which I liked at first, because I could close my eyes and imagine I was floating near a patch of honeysuckle. But the buzzing never changed pitch, which was completely unlike a real bumblebee, so I eventually called out and asked Silvia to come turn it off.

She grumbled about having to get up, but she reached in and flipped the switch anyway. The buzzing and the light went out at the same time, which gave me a feeling of freefall. It was as if I had been tied to a dock before, and Silvia had just cut me loose. I began to imagine I was drifting in the middle of a huge river somewhere in the tropics, a place known for its almond plantations. I could hear the distant sound of the workers' televisions, which flickered in the jungle night and scared off curious tree leopards. The Amazon sun had been cooking the river all day. The fish had been driven down to the bottom, where it was cooler, and that left the bubbly surface all to me.

I imagined I was a girl floating down that river on a raft, and then something better occurred to me. *I* was the raft, and Silvia was the girl. The river was salty here because we were very close to the sea. The saltiness of the water made Silvia happy because it meant that we were almost in California, which everyone else thought was land, but which she and I knew was really a secret ocean.

It was hard to know whether I was asleep or awake in that wonderful dark tub. Silvia finally called out to see if I was okay, and I said, "Oh my *God*." I said, "Silvia, I'm totally fine."

chapter thirteen

ilvia and I were snuggling in bed when Rosie came to get us up. She breezed right in, swept the curtains aside, and said, "It's cold in here!" She studied the thermostat for a moment, shaking her head. I thought she was going to be mad about all the electricity we had used, but when she saw Silvia and me curled up under the covers, she smiled, which made her look completely unlike a mouse. She said we had to go pretty soon.

Silvia thanked her about a million times. So did I. Before we left, Rosie gave us two bath towels and a bunch of miniature soaps and shampoos. She even offered us a Gideon Bible. Silvia said she already had a bible, but that I could probably use one. I let *that* suggestion die.

Silvia gave Rosie an awkward sideways hug, which was the best she could do on account of the belly, and then we went out to the Dodge and got back on the Beltway. There was heavy traffic because it was rush hour again, but I didn't mind. My skin was still tingling from the long bath and the nap in that cool, cool room. The sun was red and low, and the air felt good, even out there in all that traffic. We had the windows rolled down. Everybody was trapped in their cars. Silvia and I laughed at the impatience of the commuters, who were peeling in and out of lanes and shaking their fists at each other, even though the traffic was barely moving.

We finally got around to the exit for the interstate heading west, which was where we should have gotten off the Beltway the night before. Silvia headed for the ramp. She was concentrating on getting over, so she didn't notice that a State Trooper had pulled in behind us. I didn't tell Silvia about it. Some things are better to know after the fact, when knowing can't make you nervous. We weren't speeding— we couldn't have, if we wanted to, on account of the traffic—and, as far as I could tell, we weren't doing anything else wrong, either. Silvia was a fine driver, even if she didn't have a driver's license.

Then the trooper turned on his siren. I made Silvia pull over to the right, onto the shoulder, the way my grandmother always did when she heard a siren. I was hoping he'd just speed up and pass us, but he slowed down, too.

Silvia wanted to make a run for it. "He knows! He knows!" she said.

"Knows what?" I asked.

"About me. About you. The car. The house. Everything."

I tried to get her to calm down. You can't outrun a State Trooper, and besides, we hadn't done anything illegal, either one of us—at least not having to do with Silvia's driving. If you didn't count the no license thing.

We parked on the shoulder. The trooper pulled his cruiser to a stop about twenty feet behind us, jutting it out at an angle, almost into traffic. It took him forever to get out of his car. He talked on the radio for a long time, wrote some things down, and then waited, tapping on the steering wheel with his pen. Then he talked on the radio some more. Finally, he swung his door open. Everything he did was exceedingly slow, even the way he put on his hat after he got out of the car. The Beltway drivers were slowing down and rubbernecking. The trooper seemed to like that. He treated the shoulder of the highway like his stage. His incredibly slow official walk gave me plenty of time to study the goofy hat perched so high on his buzz cut. I wondered how he kept it clean in such a dusty job. That's the kind of trivial thing I tend to focus on before lying. It helps free up the rest of my mind to work on the lie itself.

I pretended to sneeze. While my mouth was covered, I told Silvia to let me do the talking.

The trooper stood by Silvia's door and tapped the roof of the Dodge. He looked out at the traffic for a moment, as if he wanted to see how full the theater was before starting his big monologue. Then he leaned over in an extremely condescending way and said, "Evening, ladies." Silvia's belly looked gigantic reflected in the curve of his mirrored sunglasses.

"What seems to be the problem, Officer?" I asked innocently. I had heard my grandmother say that once. I planned to do everything I thought she would do—within limits. My grandmother had a knack for dealing with authority figures which I definitely lacked.

The trooper didn't acknowledge me. He asked Silvia for her driver's license and the car's registration. Silvia looked very alarmed, which fit in to my plan perfectly. "Officer," I said. "I'm afraid she can't understand you." He gave me an annoyed look. So did Silvia. I took her hand in mine, as if I was about to say something very important, and blurted out some very nasal gibberish. "Muh-na-na pontish seen, poodada," I said. Of course it was complete nonsense. Silvia looked almost as surprised as the trooper.

Then I turned to him and said, "We hope there isn't a problem. We've got some pressing business at the consulate."

The trooper clicked his front teeth together, not unlike those chattering joke teeth, but quieter and slower. He said, "The consulate. Uh huh."

"Did we do something wrong, Officer?" I said.

The trooper looked away again at the traffic. "Routine stop, Ma'am. I'd like to see some registration and a driver's license." I pretended to translate for Silvia. She didn't know what to do, so she just listened with an expression of disbelief on her face. I turned to the trooper. He was clicking his teeth again. "I'd like to introduce you to the wife of the Portuguese consul," I said, indicating Silvia. "She's having contractions. We're on our way to the consulate, to pick up her husband—the consul—and then go to the hospital."

Of course, if the trooper knew any *real* Portuguese, the whole plan was sunk, but I figured he had less of a chance of knowing Portuguese than Spanish, which is why I chose it. The trooper didn't say anything. I wished I could tell what was going on behind those mirrored glasses. It was like dealing with an insect.

Silvia started to play along. She squeezed her belly and moaned a little. Then she tried out some of her own gibberish, which sounded much more authentic because of her Spanish accent. The trooper waited for my translation. Silvia went on and on. When she finally finished, I said, "The consul's wife appreciates the fine job you troopers are doing. She says that the consul is very supportive of local law enforcement. She also says that if we don't go right now, she's going to have the baby right here in the front seat." I leaned across her to confide in the trooper. "I think you should know," I whispered, "that having a baby in a car is like the biggest humiliation imaginable among the ruling classes. In Portugal."

The trooper was silent. I couldn't see his eyes, but he seemed to be scoping out Silvia's cheap dress and the front seat full of trash from the Mini-Mart. Suddenly he excused himself. He said he wanted to check something out.

It was a very bad sign. On the way back to his cruiser, he paid special attention to our license plate. Then it occurred to me: I hadn't considered diplomatic tags!

The lie was unraveling. I said, "Quick, the fizzy water." Silvia handed me the bottle. I used my teeth on the cap, since my wrist was useless. As soon as I got the top off, I started dumping water in Silvia's lap.

"Hey! It's cold! Stop that," she said.

"Let it soak in," I said. "I'm serious. Trust me." I reached over, elbowed the horn, and started waving. I was watching the trooper in the side view mirror. He had stopped next to his cruiser. His legs were bowed, as if he had just climbed down off a horse. He twisted his body, which pulled his jacket away from his gun. I hoped that exposing his gun was just a habit and nothing that he had thought through. I kept honking and waving, thinking: *Come on, cowboy. Over here.*

When the trooper was within earshot, I shouted, "Her water broke! The baby's coming!" He took a good long look at Silvia's wet lap. Then he pinched the brim of his hat and said, "I'm giving you ladies an escort to City General. Follow me."

*   *   *

*   *

chapter fourteen

The drive to the hospital was very fast. There was no such thing as a red light or a stop sign. It was weird, not worrying about getting caught. At times, the trooper would slow down and make sure that we were still with him. He even waved to us once or twice. You wouldn't think it would matter, but those friendly waves took almost all the pleasure out of the ride.

It reminded me of the time Dad got me out of school early to go on vacation. He pulled me out of class, telling my teacher he needed me back on the farm. He used a hick voice. He had mussed up his hair and was chewing on his big beard. My teacher gave me a sympathetic look and said, "Certainly, Mr. Wilder." Dad was just having fun, but I got very self-conscious. When we were out in the hall, he made us tip-toe and sneak around corners, as if we were escaping from school, instead of just leaving it. I remember playing along, but thinking the game was silly, because how could I enjoy doing anything wrong if Dad was the ringleader?

I was hoping to get rid of the trooper as soon as we got to the hospital, but he was determined to be a hero. He ran around threatening the nurses, saying, "I have a woman in labor here who's diplomatic." It was probably the highpoint of his career.

My Portuguese consul lie worked out even better than planned. The nurses took us right into the examination area instead of making us sit in the crowded waiting room. Silvia was having a grand old time.

They gave her the best wheelchair in the house. From the airs she put on, you would have thought she really *was* the consul's wife. I told her not to say anything and to pretend not to understand English, but that didn't stop her from waving to all the sick people from her rolling throne.

The nurse asked the trooper if we needed a translator. I butted in and said, no, that the consul's wife was happy to use my services as translator, but that we would like a private room, if possible, with cable TV, because the consul's wife liked to watch CNN to catch up on news from her homeland. "There's been a lot of domestic turmoil," I added. The domestic turmoil was a nice touch, the kind of detail that comes out of nowhere when a lie's going well.

I thanked the trooper for all his help and asked him, as politely as I could, if he wouldn't mind leaving us now. I told him that the consul's wife found the sight of men in uniforms upsetting. "The revolution has just devastated the family," I said. "I hope you'll understand." The trooper said he understood perfectly. He told me how lucky he thought the consul's wife was to have an assistant like me. He was about to ask me how old I was—I could practically see the question forming on his lips—so I saluted him abruptly, spun around, and strutted back over to Silvia. Through my teeth, I told her to wave goodbye to the trooper and smile, which she did. You would have thought she was Queen Elizabeth.

The last we saw of the trooper was him proudly removing his dustless hat as he climbed into his cruiser. I never did learn why he had pulled us over, but since then I've heard that the police sometimes pull over Mexican drivers—just because they're Mexican.

✴⁎✴

Silvia and I got a private room, which made me feel a little guilty, but I figured we needed one as much as anybody. A black nurse with a nasty expression and a glittery white streak in her hair helped install Silvia in the bed. The bed was remote controlled. It whirred when the nurse pressed the button. For some reason, the nurse's hair, together with the sound of the bed machinery, reminded me of *Bride of Frankenstein,* like she was raising Silvia through the laboratory roof during a big lightning storm to try to bring her back to life. I imagined Silvia's baby starring in the sequel, where a little monster with baby neck bolts and owlish black rings around his eyes pops out of his undead Mom. I guess you could say I was feeling a little loopy.

Before the nurse left, she turned to me and said, "You ought to get that wrist looked at," which surprised me, because I hadn't noticed her looking at it. I'm usually sensitive to things like that.

There wasn't much to do until the doctor arrived. Silvia and I started bickering about what to do next. I said "stay." Silvia said "go." She was determined to get to California. I told her she'd be insane to leave. Now that we were here, she should stay and have her baby. Just then, the doctor came in. His tousled red hair and heavily freckled nose made him look more like a chemistry student than a doctor, but he already had the self-absorbed look that even very young doctors have, which probably comes from people caring so much about their opinion. He unclipped a pen from his plastic pocket protector and made a few notes on Silvia's chart. It struck me as extremely arrogant to write something down on a patient's chart before you even said "hello" to her.

The doctor nodded to me and then went right up to Silvia and offered his hand, which was very soft and white, greeting her with a phrase in a language which I didn't know. If I had to guess, I'd say it was Portuguese. He looked very proud of himself. He was a little taken aback when Silvia smiled at him awkwardly and I answered him in English, as if his Portuguese had been atrocious and we were hoping to spare him some embarrassment. He apologized and introduced himself—in English—as Dr. Locke. He didn't ask us to call him "Everett," which was the name printed on his ID badge.

I asked Dr. Locke to please forgive the consul's wife because she'd been through a lot that morning and was very shy with strangers. He gave me an odd look, but he nodded respectfully and showed Silvia his bare hands, like a magician, so there'd be no surprises when he started his exam. I was sort of curious about the examination itself, but Dr. Locke asked me to step outside for a few minutes. I apologized and said that that wouldn't be possible. "Suit yourself," he said. He pulled the curtain around the bed, leaving me all alone in the middle of the room. I suppose I should have given Silvia her privacy, but I stayed very quiet and tried to overhear what was going on anyway. At one point, Dr. Locke pronounced the word "ultrasound" very distinctly. Then I heard a high pitched "whoosh whoosh whoosh," like tiny windshield wipers. It was the baby's heartbeat!

When the examination was finished, Dr. Locke pulled back the curtain but didn't step away from Silvia's bed. He had a reluctant expression, like a person who's just finished a long hot shower and doesn't want to step out into a chilly bathroom. Then he came up very close to me and asked if we could speak privately. I told him he could say what he had to say in English, because the consul's wife wouldn't understand, but he said he preferred to talk with me alone and asked if I wouldn't mind stepping out into the hallway with him.

As soon as we were in the hallway and the door to the room was closed, Dr. Locke asked me who I was, exactly.

"In what sense?" I said, ignoring the sudden gush of acid in my stomach. When someone is fishing for information, particularly about an elaborate lie, I've learned that the thing to do is to stay cool, and always answer a question with a question.

"Are you a member of her family?"

"Why? Is there something wrong?"

"Not really," he said. "Let me ask you. Were you with her when the water broke?"

"Is it the baby? I knew I should have brought her here sooner."

Dr. Locke had been clicking and unclicking his ballpoint pen. Now he put it to the cleft of his upper lip and started to tap. "You didn't see her water break," he said. "*Did* you."

I raised what was left of my eyebrows, as if to ask, "*Should* I have seen it?"

"That's what I was afraid of. You see, the consul's wife…her water hasn't actually broken, which is worrisome in itself, because she's overdue, to the point where it might be prudent to operate." He paused for a moment and looked at his clipboard. "Frankly," he said, "I'm more concerned with the story she made up. About her water breaking."

"The story?"

"I think she faked it. My guess would be with something lime, judging from the smell."

"How bizarre!"

"Is there a history of—I know this may be delicate, but it's very important for guiding our next steps. Is there a history of depression or mental illness in the family? I'm not saying that there absolutely has to be something like that. I just need to know."

I pretended to think back. "Now that you mention it, I did hear something once."

"Yes?"

"Something mental health related. But I can't put my finger on it. You know, I think it would be best if we asked the consul's wife directly, don't you?"

"Yes," he said. "That might be best." He put his pen away slowly, like someone putting down a racket after losing a tennis match. He stood for a moment with his hand on the door, tapping the metal plate with the side of his thumb. "Know what?" he said. "I could use a consult on this one. I'll be back in a few minutes."

Then he bowed to me, which was very formal and out of place, and walked away. He was almost through the double doors to the waiting room when he called back over his shoulder, "And I'm going to take a look at that wrist of yours when I get back. A fracture like that could cost you your hand." I smiled and waved toodleloo, but I didn't like what he said about my wrist. Not one bit.

Back in the room, Silvia had the TV on. She was watching the local news.

"Oh my God, Chica, you have to see this," she said. "It's about you and me."

chapter fifteen

* * *
* *

Everyone knows that the news on TV is phony. Try flipping from channel to channel at five thirty or six o'clock. Or eleven. All the different channels show exactly the same news stories, in exactly the same order, night after night. Talk about a conspiracy. Not to mention those hypnotized anchors with their robotic banter.

If I had any doubts that the so-called "news" was completely made up, the story they told about me and Silvia convinced me. I remember it almost word for word, because it was all so outrageous and false. The black anchorman with the buck teeth—the one my grandfather always called "Mr. Beaver"—read it, in that fumbling anchorman way, like a five year old:

"In a bizarre twist on a story we brought you several days ago, the alleged kidnapper of local school girl Chloe Wilder has been positively identified as illegal alien Silvia Morales. The suspect was seen by fire-fighters early this morning fleeing the scene of an explosion at the girl's foster home. The girl's grandparents, whose house was rocked by a huge fireball, claim that Ms. Morales is mentally unbalanced, and angry at being forced from the home, where she worked as a domestic until she was recently fired. No one was injured in the blast. The resulting fire was quickly brought under control. Police are asking anyone who has seen either Silvia Morales or Chloe Wilder to please call the number on your screen. Ms. Morales should be considered extremely danger-ous. The two were last seen in a stolen white Dodge Aries K…"

They showed the license number of my grandparents' Dodge. Then they showed a picture of me, the one from the Field School that was on the milk cartons. It looked even less like me on TV than on a sweaty milk carton, which was something at least. They didn't have a photograph of Silvia, which goes to show how temporary her life was at my grandparents'. Instead of a photograph, they had a police sketch. The eyebrows were thick and angry. The lips were huge. The expression on the face was more like a terrorist than a maid. The sketch had my grandfather written all over it.

The other channels were showing our story, too. I didn't even have to check to know that, but I checked anyway.

The rest of what they said about us on the news was unimportant, but I do remember that right after Mr. Beaver finished reading his lies, he and the other anchorman joked about how badly some sports team was doing, comparing their bad season to the explosion at my grandparents' house. That's when I turned off the TV.

Silvia and I sat there in the room, which was quiet now, except for the regular chirp of Silvia's heartbeat from one of the monitors. We tried to kid each other about the police sketch. It might have been funny, in different circumstances.

Silvia hadn't understood the story word for word, so I went over it with her, which was much more painful than just watching it on TV.

"Your grandparents think I kidnapped you? And exploded their house?" she said. I nodded and said that they could be pretty stupid at times. Silvia started to cry. She said, "I thought they *liked* me." It amazed me that her feelings could be so hurt after all my grandparents had done to her.

Silvia sat quietly for a while trying to calm her mind. Finally she asked, "What does this mean for us?" I told her it meant that we couldn't use the car any more, because now the police would be looking for it.

"And we have to leave the hospital?" I'm not the easiest person to move emotionally, but I leaned over and gave her a hug when she asked that. I even cried a little. Hearing the baby's heartbeat had obviously made her want to stay.

"Now more than ever," I said.

Silvia sat at the edge of the bed for a long time. Her lips were trembling. I helped pull the rubber suckers off her belly. The monitor squealed. "Then let's go," she said. "Roberto says the California hospitals are good, too."

After that, there wasn't time to be sappy. I helped Silvia out of her hospital gown and back into her street clothes. The fizzy water had dried in one big faded blotch. Silvia noticed it, although I was hoping she wouldn't. She started experimenting with the hospital gown, pinching it in back, examining the hems. I could tell she was considering wearing it, even though it was made out of paper. She told me it was quite nice. That's the exact expression she used: "This is quite nice." I told her to forget about the paper gown. My exact expression was: "You're wasting our time with that piece of trash." I didn't mean to be nasty, but my words hung in the air afterwards like a bad smell.

The scotch tape had come off my fingers, and I couldn't feel them very well any more, which worried me, but at least there was less pain. I went though all the drawers in the room, hoping to find something for my wrist. One drawer was full of neatly rolled Ace bandages. Each roll was clamped with a pair of little toothy clips. I grabbed a few rolls. Then I hit the jackpot: a drawer with slings and arm braces. I tried some on. The only one that came close to fitting was covered with pictures of lacrosse sticks and helmets and the words "Go Team!" It screamed "stupid jock," but it fit, so I strapped it on. I also picked up some Band-Aids, and a few tongue depressors. I didn't know what I was going to do with the tongue depressors, but I just couldn't resist. They were so clean and smooth and practical-looking.

Then we left, sneaking through the halls like the thieves we were. Silvia insisted we go to the car and try to get the bag of food from the Mini-Mart. She said she wasn't going on any more trips without real food, and since I had basically just evicted her from her hospital room, I didn't argue. It turned out I was right about losing the car, though. When we got to the level of the parking garage where the trooper had parked our car for us, the elevator doors opened on a major crime scene, complete with tons of flashing police lights and news cameras. I shoved Silvia over to the side of the elevator and pressed the "Close Door" button about fifty times before we were on our way back up to the lobby.

The only way out of the hospital that didn't have a policeman stationed at it was the loading dock. It took us almost an hour to find it. By then, I practically had to carry Silvia. She was beginning to look defeated. I couldn't admit that at the time. I remember telling myself it was probably all her hormones.

chapter sixteen

Ours is a city of poor neighborhoods. Most of them aren't so bad, unless you happen to be talking to my grandparents. If you listened to them, you'd think that everything inside the Beltway—except for two or three blocks right around their house—was practically Sodom. My grandparents are the kind of people who lock their doors as soon as they see a black person. They'll be riding along in the car, and suddenly, "Thunk!", the automatic locks go down. My grandfather won't announce it, but you just know he's mentally reporting the sighting: "Danger. Black man, nine o'clock!" What he'll say out loud is: "This used to be a nice neighborhood."

Locking your doors like that could be a silly, totally racist thing to do. Around City General, though, it made some sense. This was a truly bad neighborhood. Most of the shootings you heard about on the news happened near City General. The hospital was famous for its emergency room. The TV news people loved to say the words, "Shock Trauma," which is what the emergency room was called. You couldn't stand on the sidewalk here and not think of those words. You couldn't walk down the street and not wish you were in a car with locked doors.

It was cool out. There was a foul breeze. A police cruiser crawled down the street like a well fed beetle, shining its spotlight into the peeling doorways and the filthy crevasses between buildings. Silvia and I kept ahead of it, trying every door, except where we had to climb over a sleeping person. The whole neighborhood seemed locked up tight and abandoned, as if an invasion was coming, or already had come. There were padlocked iron fences in front of all the stores, and I began to feel that the street was a kind of jail, only instead of being locked *in*, Silvia and I were locked *out*, which amounted to the same thing. The police cruiser was still rolling along. It was slowly catching up with us.

We finally found an unlocked door. It was a barbershop, with an old fashioned red, white, and blue sign outside. The sign wasn't lit or spinning, so I thought the place might be closed, but then I saw a barber inside, an old guy with a spiky flattop and a shriveled red nose. A loud buzzer sounded when I opened the door, which surprised me. I don't know what I was expecting. Maybe jangling bells.

The barber stood between the two red barbershop chairs, the nice old kind with leather and pretty metal, with one hand resting on each, as if the chairs were his kneeling servants, ready to attack at a single quiet word. A ceiling fan squealed crookedly above his head, its blades black with grime. I smelled pomade and cigars and cooking grease.

The barber growled at Silvia.

"Men only," he said. Then he unfolded a big rubbery apron, shook some hair off it, and held it up as if he was a bullfighter. "Well?" he said to me. I wanted to get out of there, but the cruiser was still lurking outside, its flashing blue lights reflecting endlessly in the barbershop mirrors. The barber balanced his sodden cigar on the edge of an ashtray. "You want a cut or what?"

He thought I was a boy!

"Okay," I said. "Yeah, whatever," I added, in case the "okay" sounded too girlish.

"Your girlfriend'll have to wait over there," the barber said, jabbing at Silvia with his fingers, which still looked like they were holding an invisible cigar. Silvia obviously wanted to leave, but I said, "She won't mind. You've got magazines."

"The ladies do like their magazines," said the barber. "What'll it be?"

I didn't know what to say. I had never had a boy's haircut before.

"I don't know," I said. "Something different." Apparently, that was exactly the wrong thing to say, because a look of disgust spread over the barber's pug face. He wrapped a paper towel around my neck and then buttoned the apron around it—much tighter than he had to.

"Okay pretty boy," he said, snorting. "Just tell me. You want a Zero, a One, or a Two Point Five?"

I thought about that for a while. It seemed like a big decision. The barber got impatient. "Don't tell me you want a Four," he said. A Four seemed like a bad thing, so I shook my head and said "How about a One?" A One sounded better than a Zero, which I figured was the opposite of a Two Point Five and possibly as undesirable as a Four.

"Now we're getting somewhere," the barber said. "A One it is." He plugged in a big electric tool that looked like a hedge clipper. Then he stood behind me and looked at me in the mirror as if my head were a lump of clay. He tugged at my hair disapprovingly and said, "Who did this, a lawnmower?" He was being needlessly rude, and I felt like telling him off, but he looked like the kind of person you'd have to explain your sarcasm to, which takes all the fun out of it, so I just said, "No, I was in a play."

"A play, huh? Interesting," the barber said. "Velly intelesting." He put on a smudged pair of reading glasses, leaned over to a round wire rack on his counter, and spun it slowly, as if he was roasting a suckling pig. "Let's see. A Zero. A Two Point Five. A Triple Zero. A Four. Hello. What have we here?" he said. He turned and gave me a significant look. "A One." It was a tiny black plastic comb, just like all the other tiny black plastic combs on the rack. He took off his glasses, set them back down, and then dipped the One into a glass dish full of blue liquid. He dipped in the One several times, studying the blue film which formed momentarily across the plastic teeth, then dunking it completely and stirring it around the bottom of the dish with his hairy pinkie. When he was finished with that, he dried the One on a stained washcloth tucked in his belt. "That'll git it," he said, clipping the One to the electric tool. "Now, let's cut some hair."

I'm not saying that I go to fancy hair salons like my grandmother, but in the past, the person cutting my hair had always used scissors. It was strange to feel the hedge clippers going through my hair. The vibrations tickled my teeth. The barber hummed a song while he was cutting, but he had an awful voice, full of cigar phlegm.

I watched long strips of hair peel over my forehead and fall into the apron. It reminded me of a TV show I had seen once about the wool harvest. Sheep cowboys squeezed the trembling sheep between their legs and ran electric shears all over their bodies. I had been amazed by the sheep's enormous black eyes, which followed the path of the shears, as if they understood what was being done to them but couldn't fathom why anyone would do it.

My head was a lot smaller than a whole sheep. It only took a few strokes with the shears to take off all my hair. It was even a pleasant feeling, a kind of lightening, which I might have been able to enjoy if I hadn't been so fixated on the word "baldy." After my hair was gone, the barber slathered the back of my neck with hot shaving cream, which he got from a crusty electric dispenser on the counter. He took up a straight razor—the horror movie kind that swings open and has absolutely no safety features—and flicked it back and forth for a while against a leather strap.

I have to admit that having the back of my neck shaven felt great—the combination of the hot lather and the cool air on my freshly shaven neck added to the nice gentle scratching of the razor. The barber slapped on some green liquid when he was done, which stung but gave off a nice pine tree smell, and then he stood behind me, holding up a hand mirror. I didn't really want to look, but the barber made me. What I saw didn't look like me, not in the least. I said, "Wow, great." Then he finally put the hand mirror down.

Now I absolutely looked like a boy.

I caught Silvia looking at me in the mirror. She had been pretending to read an old girlie magazine. "It looks good," she said, trying to stifle a laugh. "No, really." It was almost worth looking like a boy to see her smile again.

"The jury has spoken," the barber said, sweeping the apron off my lap. "Course, now there's less to hang onto." I didn't know exactly what that meant, but it was definitely not nice. He said it quietly, as if I had just joined a secret club, which, being a boy now, I guess I had.

"How much?" I asked.

"Seven plus tip," he said. I gave him a ten dollar bill and waited for the change but he just closed the register and said, "We thank you for your business."

It was time to go. The whole haircut had taken five minutes.

Silvia slipped her arm through mine when we were back outside. "My new boyfriend," she said, laughing. I told her to cut it out, but as we walked along and I caught sight of my square head reflected in the soaped-up storefronts, I started to pretend I really was a boy. I swallowed a lot of air and belched. Silvia said that was gross, so I did it again, this time saying her name while burping. Afterwards, I said,

"Nice one," the way boys do after a juicy burp. "Check this out," I said, swaggering along and scratching my armpits.

"You're a boy, not a monkey," Silvia said. "Boys don't walk like that. They do it like this." She leaned back as she walked, her hands stiff and bent at the wrist, like a praying mantis. She was trying to look like a black street boy. "With attitude," she said. She frowned and tried to look tough. Her big belly made the whole thing ridiculous.

The streets were just as empty as before, only for some reason they didn't feel quite so threatening. Maybe it was being a boy, but I wasn't even scared when three chained Rotweilers started barking at us from behind a fence. They were low, thick-necked dogs, with plenty of saliva in their chops. I stopped in front of them and bowed—from the waist. I pretended to tip an imaginary hat. "Boys," I said—I figured that anything that drooled like that had to be male —"don't make me come in there and kick your ass."

Silvia pulled me away from the dogs, typical of a girl. She fluffed my buzz-cut. "Well, Mister, what do we call you?" she said.

I thought about it for a minute. Names are serious. They can make or break what you think about yourself.

"Call me Finn," I said.

Silvia had trouble pronouncing it. She made it sound Mexican. "Finn" came out "Feen." "Feen *what?*" she said.

"Just Finn," I said. "Like 'Cher.' Or 'Sting.'"

"Only one name? It's strange."

An elevated train roared overhead, shooting off blue sparks like a wind-up toy. I watched the train until it disappeared around a corner a few blocks away. The way it curved down and away was beautiful, like something you'd do with your arm to mimic a bird. For some reason, Silvia and I started to talk about California again as if it was still a real possibility. After a block or two of dreamy chatter, I had to stop. Silvia was obviously getting her hopes up. I finally told her that, as a practical matter, there was no way we could make it to California.

"Finn, you're wrong," she said, pointing at the ramp in the middle of the street where the elevated tracks came back down to the ground. We were near the end of the line. I had been so wrapped up in being a boy that I hadn't noticed how far we had come—right up to the edge of the railroad yard.

Silvia ran her fingers through my prickly hair and said, "We'll take a train."

chapter seventeen

I had never seen a railroad yard at night, at least not from the ground. It was a place of the harshest light and the deepest black. I felt x-rayed under the yellow crime lights but invisible everywhere else. The power lines overhead hummed like cannibals. Signs everywhere said "Danger! Electrocution Hazard!", to the point where I jumped every time I brushed up against something.

An elevated highway towered over one edge of the yard on white concrete legs. I couldn't see any on-ramps or exits, just the highway itself, swooping across the downtown skyline like the path to a forbidden city.

I climbed as high as I could on a crumbling stone block wall. Every surface I touched was black—the stones, the metal, even the craggy outcroppings of rock—as if the friction of the trains' endless comings and goings over the years had scorched everything. A monster freight train rumbled by, its bell tolling. I started counting the cars, but stopped at fifty-eight. I never got used to the way the ground shook under its wheels, as if the train was trying to pound the earth back to life.

Silvia waited for me at the bottom of the stone wall. She was pressing her back into it, flattening herself, even though the train was passing at least twenty feet away. I understood her fear. It was easy to imagine you could drown in the train's wake.

After it passed, I jumped down and said, "Those are some big machines."

Silvia said, "They're quite nice inside, probably." We spent a reassuring minute brushing soot off each other.

I wanted to discourage Silvia. "The railroad yard is a mess," I said. "Tracks everywhere. Too many trains. It looks dangerous." The thought of Silvia running for a moving train made me wince, because I couldn't separate the picture of her running from the picture of her tripping on a stone and hitting her belly on the rails.

"What about the trains for California?" she asked.

"They don't put signs on them," I said. "Besides, we don't have enough money for the train."

"Then we'll take the other kind," she said.

"What kind?"

"The kind you don't pay for. Like this one." We had to stop talking for a moment while the roaring engine of another freight train passed.

"Forget it," I said. "Do you have any idea who rides those things? Criminals. Hobos. People who like begging and murder."

"Oh, come on. That's not everybody. Good people ride them, too." She was getting a new tone in her voice, like someone in a lot of pain who's managing to rise above it. She sounded almost saintly.

"Well, you obviously know everything," I said. Then I started looking for a way into the yard, so I wouldn't have to stand there and feel like a big baby.

If I'd been willing to walk along the tracks, we could have strolled right in with the trains. Silvia suggested it. It was tempting, because the trains were moving nice and slow, but I absolutely refused. The speed of things at night can be very deceptive, and there were places along the tracks where you couldn't just step out of the way when the trains came through.

There were tall fences everywhere, and plenty of razor wire, but the fences were old and mostly for show. I found a place where Silvia could walk right through a gap in the chain link and not have to climb over or under anything.

As confusing as the yard looked from the top of a stone wall, it was a thousand times worse when you were sneaking around the tracks, because your view was blocked everywhere by trains or little houses or the sinister humming electricity towers. Trains were rolling in and out all the time, which was terrifying enough by itself, but even worse considering that each time a train arrived or left, the layout of the yard changed. It was like being on a stage with people constantly moving the set around. We never knew where we were. I didn't like climbing under the trains, either. The rims of those enormous steel wheels gleamed like steak knives.

I was scared, and ready to lash out at Silvia when she said, "Finn, look! California!" She pointed out a forlorn looking chain of boxcars.

I had to hand it to her. The name painted on the sides of the cars was "California Pacific."

The boxcars were all padlocked. Silvia tried all the doors anyway, until she found one we could open. It had a padlock but wasn't really locked. The latch must have been broken. She was so excited when I opened the door, you would have thought the boxcar was her dream house. It was dry and roomy inside. The floors and walls were smooth wood planks. I saw how much Silvia liked it, but I wasn't giving in so easily. "I don't know," I said. "It's kind of a mess." But Silvia ignored me. She went right for the metal rungs and tried to claw her way up. I stood back for a while and let her go at it. I wanted her to ask for my help. She managed to get halfway to the second rung before she had to stop and catch her breath. She was sweating and gasping for breath.

Her thigh muscles were trembling.

"Wow. It's slippery," she said, as if the rungs were the problem.

"Yeah," I said, giving her an upward shove, "it's definitely not your big fat belly."

As soon as we were inside, Silvia started straightening up the place. She made a bed out of some plastic sheeting and a few Colorado newspapers. Seeing her work so hard made me guilty, so I swept the floor a little with the side of my sneaker.

Silvia settled down on her new nest. She rolled onto her side and asked me for help packing some crumpled newspaper around her belly for support, like when gardeners pack straw around a prize pumpkin to keep it from rolling away. I tried not to jostle her too much. Then I sat down with her. Somehow, her head made its way into my lap.

I didn't completely approve of the boxcar, or the freight train idea in general, but I found myself stroking Silvia's hair with my good hand anyway. She closed her eyes and told me it felt nice. Then she told me that she hadn't slept outside since crossing the border into Texas. She said how much she liked night air. I wanted to tell her she wasn't sleeping outside, but I got the feeling she was talking just for the sake of talking.

While she was lying in my lap, I realized I didn't know very much about Silvia's life before she came to my grandparents' house. She had been there when I arrived, and I always thought of her as a fixture, like the refrigerator or the big comfy glider on the porch—something practically built in. I just assumed she had been there forever. Actually, back then I didn't think about her much at all. I was pretty focused on my own problems.

I asked Silvia what it was like crossing the border. She started by telling me that she had always heard awful things about the States, which surprised me because I always assumed that foreigners couldn't wait to get here. I'd be the first to say that life in America isn't exactly the greatest all the time, but I'd always imagined it was worse in other countries, especially in Mexico, with all the poverty. At least that's what I'd heard.

But according to Silvia, she was happy living in her Mexican town, which was actually a good-sized city. I kept asking her questions about it, like did they have buses and cabs, and was there an airport, etc. Silvia thought my questions were funny. She said I sounded like a Mexican trying to find out about America. I would have been insulted by that, coming from anyone else.

Anyway, Silvia was happy to stay down in Mexico, but things changed when her mother died and her father started having health problems. I asked if he had gotten bitten by a tarantula, or if his lungs had been ruined in a silver mine, but Silvia laughed and said no, he just had high blood pressure, and it was getting more and more difficult for him to do his job as a civil engineer. This created a problem for his daughters, because they had gotten into the habit of spending a lot of money, using their credit cards—credit cards!—too much. One night, their father sat them down and spoke to them about money problems. Silvia was the oldest of three sisters. She said she decided then and there to leave to make it easier on her sisters, who were still in high school.

All this talk of life in Mexico was a little bewildering to me, especially the details, which didn't sound all that exotic. In fact, I envied the life Silvia was describing, on account of the sisters, and the credit cards, and a father who sat down with you to explain serious things. I said it must have been hard to leave, and Silvia said it was, but there wasn't much choice. The family needed money, and there weren't any jobs in her city, at least not for her. Mexico was pretty chauvinistic when it came to work. They gave priority to men. Her sisters' weddings were going to be expensive, and so was taking care of her father. I didn't ask Silvia about her own wedding. It was obvious that she had put the idea of getting married behind her. Suddenly, Roberto and his stuffed animals seemed a lot less ridiculous. No—they were still ridiculous, but in my mind, Silvia's doomed feelings for Roberto made her more noble.

So she decided to come to the States. When I asked her why she didn't just do it legally, she laughed and told me it was almost impossible. The legal way involved some kind of lottery. Tons of people entered it, and besides, they gave preference to people with special skills. I told her I thought she was very skilled. She thanked me, but said they meant *skilled,* as in mechanic or animal doctor.

She decided to do it illegally. First she tried with the help of a cousin who promised to sneak her in safely, but he turned out to be a crook. He never showed up where they agreed to meet, so Silvia had to hire someone else, called a "wolf," to help her across the border, which is how the very poorest and most desperate Mexicans do it.

The crossing itself took almost two weeks. During that time, there was almost no food or water. Even going to the bathroom was a big ordeal because everyone had to stay hidden in the back of a truck all the time. It was the first time Silvia had been in close quarters with "peasants," as she called them, which I guess meant Mexican people even poorer than her. She said that the peasants kept to themselves, except when they were on her case about being a snob. The part about her being called a snob amazed me. Who ever heard of a Mexican snob?

Finally, it was time to cross the river. It had been raining for several days, and the river was swollen. Silvia's wolf had told everyone to stay put, because the river was too dangerous to cross, but Silvia was getting suspicious, because every day they waited, the people in her group got a little weaker. The wolf was starting to pay too much attention to her. He had already demanded to spend the night with two of the peasant girls. No one could stop him. He threatened to kill anyone who didn't do what he said, but no one really believed him. It was simpler than that. They just couldn't afford to turn back.

One night, the wolf went to buy liquor. That night was going to be Silvia's turn with him. She told the others it was now or never. Half the group wanted to stay, but the rest were for going, including the two peasant girls the wolf had already raped. The ones who wanted to go, went. Silvia led the way.

They crossed at night. The river wasn't anywhere near as bad as the wolf had said. At least that's what Silvia thought at first. But when they counted heads on the other side, they discovered that one of the peasant girls was missing. Her father said it was probably a blessing, since she had been ruined by the wolf anyway. You can imagine what the other ruined girl felt on hearing that. Silvia sort of adopted her from then on because her family was starting to turn its back on her. "You met that girl," Silvia said. "Rosaria. From the hotel."

Things didn't get much easier once they were on the U.S. side, because then they were spotted by the border patrol, which chased them with guns and motorcycles. Some of the Mexicans got caught and sent back, so all their suffering was for nothing. Silvia got away, but she was alone now. It took three more days for her to find a church that would help her and not tell the authorities. Eventually, she made her way up north through an underground railroad, and wound up at my grandparents' house. She was grateful to them—even now—but she still hadn't earned a single dollar to send back to her family.

We sat for a while not speaking, just listening to the trains, which sounded like suitcases being dragged down the halls of a cheap motel.

I told Silvia I thought she was extremely brave. I told her she should never, ever be a maid again, although I secretly doubted it was possible. After that, I had to move because my legs were giving me pins and needles, and when I transferred Silvia's head from my lap to a little newspaper pillow, I saw that she was sound asleep. She probably hadn't heard a word I said.

chapter eighteen

* *
    *
  * *

The jolt came just before morning. I was expecting a big clank-
ing collision, because that's what it sounded like from the outside when they rammed train cars together. But this was extra
gentle, as if they knew that Silvia was snoring away and really needed
her sleep. There was a nudge up at the front of the train, and then the
distant metallic kiss of the cars hooking up. My sleepy mind interpreted it as a kiss on the cheeks, as if everything was finally beginning
to come together, and not just the train.

I woke Silvia up. It wasn't easy. She was curled up tight, her arms
wrapped around her belly, as if the night had turned her into a moth-
ering ball. While she was still groggy, I put my hand on her belly and
felt the baby kicking. She was very happy when I told her we were
almost on our way. She stretched out like a cat and said she wouldn't
mind staying in bed all day. I told her I thought that was a good plan.

After ten minutes, though, we still hadn't felt an encouraging
lurch, or even the powerful grumble of the engine being started. After
half an hour, Silvia asked me if we were going soon.

"Do I look like a train schedule?" I asked.

"Chica, I have to pee." It surprised me to hear her call me
"Chica." I guess I was getting used to "Finn."

"Well, you can't just pee in the corner," I said.

"And I agree with you," Silvia said.

"But it's light outside. People can see."

"Let them. It's a natural function."

"I mean the police," I said, which shut her up.

Then I noticed something. There was a sort of sliding hatch in the corner of the boxcar, near the floor, about the size and shape of a pet door.

"Come here and give me a hand," I said. The two of us managed to slide the hatch up along its wooden tracks. I half expected a dog to come trotting in.

The hatch opened onto a black stone wall. No one would be able to see what we were doing.

"Welcome to the ladies' room," I said.

"And the men's room," Silvia said.

The sliding door didn't stay up by itself, so I had to hold it there while Silvia went through the ordeal of gathering up her skirt, pulling down her underwear, and squatting—all of it very slowly, like an old person. I waited for her to do her business.

"I can't," Silvia said, after a while.

"Why not?"

"I don't know," she said. "Maybe I'm nervous."

"Well, get over it," I said. But she couldn't. Her legs started shaking. "Out of the way," I said. "It's my turn." I didn't have any trouble with the arrangement. I wasn't nervous in the least.

Suddenly a man outside shouted, "What the hell?"

Silvia dropped the sliding hatch, which was a good move, except my ankles got splashed.

"Did I just pee on someone?" I asked.

"I think, yes," Silvia said.

"We should have looked."

"I did look. He wasn't there before."

We heard an angry voice, and then there was a knock on the box-car door. It wasn't just a straightforward "knock-knock-knock," either. It was a mixture of knuckle taps and scratching. It certainly didn't sound like a policeman's knock.

I opened the door a crack. A young toothless man with long red greasy hair in a ponytail was wringing out his socks.

"You call this civilized?" he said, holding up the socks accusingly. "Gimme some water."

"Sorry," I said. "We're all out."

The toothless man spat. He was muttering about people who peed on you and then didn't even have the courtesy to share their water. I couldn't help staring at his turned-in, old man lips. His mouth looked ancient compared to the rest of him, which was wiry and sunburnt and strong. He was wearing a cheap plastic poncho, the kind that folds up into a tiny envelope.

"This isn't a barnyard, where animals go around urinating on each other," he said. I'd never heard of a barnyard where animals did that, but I said, "Sorry, we didn't know. I'm Finn. And this is Silvia."

"Business first. Then the niceties," he said, forcing the door open a little wider. I tried to stop it from sliding, but he was very strong. He grimaced as he forced it open, his gray gums widening, as if the sliding door was somehow connected to his jaw. Then he sprang up into the boxcar, crouching for a few seconds after he landed. "You can close the door now," he said. I didn't, even though it was probably a good idea.

He went over to the sliding hatch and kicked it. "So that's the culprit," he said.

"We didn't know anyone was under there," I said.

"You just *assumed*. And then you went ahead and did your nasty duty. Like a beast in the field," he said. He was getting distracted by

Silvia. She avoided looking him in the eye, but he stood over her, eyeing her belly as if it was the main course in a buffet. "Hello there, Silvia," he said. I couldn't believe I had used her real name. It was so stupid!

"Here's five dollars for some water," I said, pulling a bill out of my pocket. Doing that dislodged a wad of bills—all the change from the Mini-Mart—which tumbled down to the boxcar floor.

"So you're a man of means," he said, accepting the five dollars from me with a stiff bow. He watched me very closely as I gathered up the bills.

"Okay then," I said. "I guess that's it."

"Clark Clarkson," he announced, extending his hand, as if I had asked his name. "I'm traveling with my protégé, the rubber boy James. You'll want to meet him." Clark tightened his lips over his gray gums, rolled his tongue, and whistled. Then he shouted, "Yo, James!"

A little black boy appeared, pausing to rest his elbows on the floor before wiggling himself into the boxcar. He looked perfectly normal in terms of arms and legs, but he moved around on his belly, rolling his torso in waves, like a dolphin. His arms were crossed behind his back. He kept them out of the way as he arched his body over to Clark. He spat on Clark's shoes and proceeded to polish them with his shoulder.

"James is new to the world of street entertainment. I'm showing him the ropes."

James stopped polishing and did another trick. He balanced on his belly, lifting his calves and craning his neck backwards until the soles of his bare feet were resting on the back of his head. He had thick calluses like a ballet dancer. I wondered if he owned a pair of shoes.

"Now he's just showing off for you," Clark said. "James is still intoxicated with his power over an audience, and has yet to learn about *timing*—which, in our business, is paramount." Clark delivered a soft kick to James's legs. There wasn't much force to it—just enough to ruin his balance. James unraveled onto the floor and said, "Whatever."

Clark stuck out his tongue at James. "Ham," he said.

"Shouldn't you two be…entertaining?" I asked.

Clark scoffed at that. "There's no money in mornings," he said. "James and I are evening players." Clark yawned. He didn't bother to cover his gaping choppers with his hand. In fact, he emphasized the yawn with a little rhythmic sigh—"Yuh yuh yuh." He seemed to like watching our reactions to the sight of his disturbing mouth. Especially Silvia's. "We're coming off one of those endless nights," he said. Then he stretched himself out near Silvia's feet, ordered James to find break-fast, and fell asleep on the spot. I thought he was faking it, but then his mouth hung open and he started to snore.

"I don't think he's asleep," Silvia whispered. James overheard her. He wiggled over to the snoring Clark, sat up—his hands always behind his back, as if they were glued there—and then, with his bare toes, picked up a fat dust bunny and tickled Clark's nose with it. Clark's eyelids twitched, but he kept on snoring.

"He was right about one thing," I told Silvia. "We need food and water."

"But what if the train goes and you're not back?" It was a good question, but I could tell she was less worried about that than being alone with Clark.

"Then I'll meet you in California," I said.

James stood up on his legs, like a normal boy, and said, "They blow a whistle when they get ready to go. We'll hear it." There was something quietly reassuring about him. Silvia gave me a haughty look, as if James had just put me in my place.

James led me across the train yard as if it was his personal playground. He knew all the secret ways. We crawled through culvert pipes and under ledges. We kept close to the trains, duck-walking underneath them whenever we could. Under the commuter trains, I worried that someone would flush a toilet on my head, but James said that was dumb.

There were plenty of workers in the yard. Sometimes we got very close to them, but they never saw us. It was like James and I were on a safari, hunting the most dangerous game—railroad workers!—and getting as close as we could without disturbing the beast in his native habitat. It was kind of sad, too, because some of those workers looked pretty friendly. I was surprised by my appetite for normal conversation. Even so, I knew it wouldn't have been conversation with those men, just an alarmed, "Hey you!" before the inevitable chase.

James led us to an open manhole cover.

"Rungs is slippery, watch out," he said. His body slid down the hole like water. I followed him. It took me longer because I wasn't made out of rubber like James, plus there was my wrist.

Then we were in the basement of the train station, which was a real labyrinth, like in the Greek myths, the kind that kept you on the lookout for monster droppings and made you wish you had a big ball of string. I could have spent the rest of my life trying to figure out that maze of identical dripping concrete tunnels, but James was a very confident guide. We only had to backtrack once, and I learned later that it hadn't been a wrong turn at all. He just knew an electrical closet where they kept boxes of nice fat chalk, which he said helped him in his work on sidewalks. He gave me a demonstration, rubbing some chalk on his callused palms and holding them out for me. "Gymnasts use it, too," he said defensively, as if using chalk was a sign of weakness.

James led us to a door with a radiation symbol and the words "Fallout Shelter." So that's what the tunnels were. I felt sorry for anyone who went down there in the event of a nuclear war. Better to be vaporized.

There were metal stairs, which James said led up to the main floor. He said "main floor" the way an elevator man would, almost singing it, with the high note on "floor." I had never ridden in an elevator with an elevator man, but my grandparents talked about it constantly. The extinction of elevator men was, in their opinion, a big symbol of the downfall of civilization. It tells you something about the world they grew up in. Their idea of civilization was forcing a poor black man in an insulting round cap to ride up and down all day in an airless elevator, just so white people could have the pleasure of saying, "Seven," or "Three," or, "Lobby, please," and watching the man's immaculate white glove push the buttons.

I started to feel guilty for thinking of James as an elevator man. I overcompensated. "Good job finding the stairs," I said enthusiastically. It was an idiotic thing to say, like congratulating an Indian for knowing where the river was. I could tell James resented it.

We climbed the metal stairs in silence, the long climb made more lonely by the clanging of our feet, which echoed against the concrete walls. The stairway smelled like cooked food and mildew, the way emergency stairs in public buildings often do, but even that nauseating smell made my stomach growl. We went through two doors marked "Keep closed at all times," down a short hallway lined with dented metal office furniture, and there we were, at the edge of the station's famous dome room, craning our necks and gawking like tourists.

It was strange to come into the station that way, after crawling around in the fallout shelter and taking the emergency stairs. Everything seemed fake: the polished marble floors and the gilded statues of kneeling men holding up the world—even the hundreds and hundreds of business people using their cell phones, reading newspapers, and trying not to spill coffee on their fancy clothes. But the phoniness somehow made the place even more impressive, as if the station and everyone in it had been polished and scrubbed and dressed up just for James and me, to show savages like us the power of wealth so that we would immediately start to feel disgusted with ourselves.

It worked, too. I dusted off my shirt. James ran his fingers over his shaven head as if he were combing it, leaving four pale furrows in the stubble.

My first impulse was to lie down on one of the long curved oak benches, slide along the cool wood, and let the cricket song of expensive leather shoes lull me back to sleep. I turned around to ask James if he had ever slept in the station, but he was gone. I was on my own, at least for a while, which suited me fine.

My feet automatically moved me to the center of the station, directly under the famous dome, as if the floor was tilted towards a drain. It was oddly hushed there. When I was really little, my grandfather had tried to explain it to me, something about acoustics and domes. Standing at the center of the room, he said, was like putting on an enormous helmet which let you watch everything in silence. For some reason, I thought about God when he said that, which was exceedingly unlike me. Thinking back, it was my closest call with religion.

A sudden whiff of cinnamon rolls emptied my head. There was a pastry cart nearby, with big wooden wheels and a hooped tent over it. It was supposed to look like a covered wagon from the Old West, but what pioneer wagon ever had a boom box, or took credit cards? A dopey high school girl in a beret was waiting on people. There was a long line. She was incredibly slow because she stopped working every three seconds to put on a despicable *"Aren't I adorable?"* face. Her smile was like an applause sign. The worst part of it was that the men in line seemed to think she really was adorable. They made sure to point out the absurdly large tips they stuffed into her jar.

In spite of all that, I couldn't resist the cinnamon smell. It reached right into my stomach. Everywhere I walked seemed to lead me back to the pastry wagon. In the end, I waited in line and put up with Ms. Adorable. I ordered two pastries, one for me and one for Silvia. They cost three dollars each, and they looked much better than they tasted, but as soon as I finished mine, I scarfed Silvia's, too. I told myself that she wouldn't have liked it anyway, that it was too rich. I considered buying another one, but the beret girl, thinking I was a boy, had done a flirty thing with her eyes when I paid her. It made me want to run back down to the fallout shelter.

★ ★ ★

James was out on the sidewalk near the taxicab stand. The doors and trunks of all the cabs were wide open, as if the cabs had just been taken out of the oven and put on a rack to cool. James was doing tricks for a small audience of black drivers, a series of poses inside a tiny chalk circle he had drawn on the sidewalk. He really could bend his body in unbelievable ways. The cab drivers stood around laughing and covering their eyes and joking about James's father being a pretzel, but they were good-natured men, and when James finished, in a pose which had his chin and forearms on the sidewalk and his feet high up in the air, they gave him lots of loose change. James accepted the money gracefully, like a professional.

When we were back inside the station, I asked him what he was going to buy with his money. "Clark's beer," he said. "My shoeshine man buys it for me. I give him a dollar tip." James liked telling me about tipping a grown man. When I asked him where we could buy food and water, he looked at me as if I was insane. "You don't buy that," he said. "Unless you're stupid."

I had to go to the bathroom, and not just to pee, so I went and found the ladies' room. A bored policeman stood by the door, sniffing the air like a dog. I tried to avoid looking at him. As I got closer, he moved in front of me. He tapped the sign with the tip of his billy club. "*Ladies'* room," he said.

"Right," I said, backing away. "For ladies. What was I thinking?"

There was no door to the men's room, just a maze of tiled walls to block the view. I hesitated at the entrance. A little Mexican man in overalls rear-ended me and said, "Watch it!"

The men's room smelled a lot worse than the ladies' room, mostly, I figured, because of the open porcelain trough where the men lined up to pee. I had seen urinals before, but they were the individual kind, separated by little metal dividers to block the view of the person peeing next to you. The trough here totally lacked privacy. It was funny to see the men stare stiffly at the wall in front of them as they peed, as if some bathroom general was walking up and down the line inspecting them. I suppose they stared that way to create a sense of privacy, even if it was pretend privacy.

The toilet stalls were decrepit—corroded and stained and a disgusting mess, with strange holes gouged through the dividing walls. I finally found one with a dry seat and an empty bowl. I had never felt so naked as I did pulling down my pants in that men's room. I expected someone to kick in the stall door any second.

James was waiting for me outside the bathroom with some bulging paper bags. "Food," he said, opening one of the bags for my inspection. Inside were an apricot pastry with lipstick-y bite marks; lots of little packets of sugar; most of a fast food egg sandwich; and some candy bars still in the wrapper, meaning they were stolen. Another bag had drinks. I pulled one out, a glass bottle of half finished grapefruit juice. A cigarette butt floated in the juice. I swirled it accusingly at James.

"The rest are okay," he said. I told him I thought that eating other people's garbage was utterly revolting, but it was just something to say. I was still starving and I knew I would eat it.

Another bag had Clark's six-pack of beer in it. The bottles clinked as we walked. James said that Clark liked his beer in bottles because the cool glass felt good against his gums.

As we were sneaking back through the railroad yard, I asked James if he knew how Clark had lost all his teeth. James shrugged. "Ate a nigger's lunch in Phoenix," he said. "Got his teeth knocked out. Boom!"

"Did you see it?" I asked.

"Not in person," James said, "but I wish I did."

When we got back to the boxcar, the door was jammed. Both of us tried, but we couldn't slide it open. Then James handed me an old crowbar he found on the ground. He was very patient with me, as if he was loaning me his house keys because I'd forgotten mine. We finally slid the door open, but only a foot or so. The boxcar was dark. It took my eyes a few seconds to adjust.

"Finn!" Silvia cried.

Clark was in Silvia's corner, wrapped around her like a python.

I didn't say anything. I went over to Clark and whacked him with the crowbar, once on the elbow and then again on the side of the knee because he still wouldn't let go. "Mr. Clarkson!" I said. "Get back in your corner!" And he did, just like a scolded dog. I stood over him for a while, the crowbar raised up over my head. I enjoyed his cowering. I liked how he was pleading for me not to hit him. I liked him calling me "Man." I was angry and *strong*.

"Come on, man," he said, kicking his legs at me and pawing the air in front of his chest. "She wanted it. Bean-eaters always want it."

And then, for saying that, the crowbar came down hard on his face.

chapter nineteen

None of us could believe what I had just done.

A curved black mark appeared on Clark's cheek, as if the tip of the crowbar had been dipped in ink. It took a few seconds for the blood to start gushing. Then it came down off his chin, spattering the dusty boxcar floor in dark drops. Clark shrieked. He was too scared to be angry yet. He kept fingering his split cheek, pressing his knuckles against the lower edge of the cut. Occasionally he would wipe away some of the blood with his fingertips, as if the wound were an eye, and the blood, some kind of embarrassing teardrop. He kept asking, "Can I get some help over here?" but no one moved to help him.

I asked Silvia if she was all right. She nodded, but there was something new and formal about her. She was looking at me with disbelief and a little fear, as if I was a new person, a stranger, which was exactly how I felt. She wouldn't come near me. It made me sad, but at the same time, I felt good about protecting her. I thought: *She's had a big shock; she'll be fine in a minute.* I was being so patronizing!

James was admiring Clark's wound, shaking his head and saying, "Damn!" I didn't know what to do about Clark. I think I said something lame like, "Serves you right."

Clark was still cussing at me, but underneath I saw that he was afraid, and I was glad of it. I wanted him to fear me because now I was much more afraid of *him*, on account of how badly I had hurt his face.

His dripping wound disgusted me, but I was also strangely proud of it. I didn't bother to offer him one of my nice clean Ace bandages.

It had seemed so natural to hit him. I had never been on the other side of that before. It made me understand a little better about my past, what it's like to raise a hand against someone and really hurt them, but at the same time think you're doing the right thing.

✯*✯

But then the anger started letting go. A long freight train rumbled by, shaking us. I wished it would keep coming until it shook us to pieces. But it passed, and afterwards the only sound in the boxcar was Clark snuffling and saying, "Freakin' unbelievable!" every time he touched his face. Whatever extra strength I had felt before was now gone. The only anger left was aimed at myself, for losing it before, and now for getting weak. All I had done was make things a thousand times more dangerous for Silvia and me.

There was an aluminum taste in my mouth. I smelled the boxcar as if for the first time that day: it stank of manure and sweat. I had an impulse to drop the crowbar and throw myself at Clark's feet, to beg him to please hit me back, much harder if he wanted to. But that was impossible. I had started playing at being a boy. Now I had to keep it up, no matter what.

James was everywhere I turned. When Clark told him to fetch some napkins for his cut, James looked to me for permission first. Clark noticed him doing it.

"You'll regret that," Clark said, as much to me as to James.

"You're saying you want some more of this?" I said, shaking the crowbar at him. James said "Damn!" again and went out to see what he could find.

Silvia looked down, shaking her head. She quietly asked if she could leave.

I told her "No."

✳ ✳ ✳

We spent the rest of the day in a bizarre standoff. Clark sulked in his corner, eyeing me murderously, mopping his cut with the fresh newspaper James had brought back instead of napkins. James buzzed around Clark's wound like a hungry fly. Silvia avoided eye contact with everyone, including me. The crowbar and I kept on top of things. I didn't plan to let Clark out of my sight until the train was rolling and I could make him jump out.

We waited and waited. I sent James out every two minutes to see if our engine car was coming. Each time I asked him to go, he arched his wispy eyebrows. When he came back, the answer was always, "Uh-uh."

We distracted ourselves by eating. Without any discussion, James had moved the bags of food from Clark's corner to mine. I gave most of the good stuff to Silvia, then me, then James. Clark got whatever was left. He threw tantrums, but ate the nasty leftovers anyway.

We heard the station clock strike noon. The sound was so out of place, so civilized, that I had to laugh. The air in the boxcar was warming up. Clark moaned in his corner for a while and then napped. James and Silvia nodded off. I was sleepy, too, but I didn't dare close my eyes.

✳ ✳ ✳

The drowsier I got in that afternoon heat, the deeper I fell into confusion. While the others slept, I stared at the rings and droplets of Clark's blood in the dust. I tried to connect the bloody dots in my imagination. I kept looking for a pattern—a shape, a face, a beast from the Zodiac—something mystical that might help explain what I had done. But the harder I looked for a grand plan, the simpler it seemed: I smashed Clark's face because I wanted to and because I could.

My thoughts were spinning around like one of those thumb-driven Easter toys, the metal flower buds that spin faster and faster until the petals open, revealing a secret scene. Something was unfolding in my mind. I began to search the day for clues, looking between the cracks for the secret scene inside what had happened. Faces changed, the true faces coming through. Silvia and Clark and James melted away, leaving Mom and Dad and me in the sweltering boxcar. As I remembered the way the crowbar felt, raised in anger, my father replaced Clark at my feet. I pictured myself standing over him, listening to him whimper and say he was sorry, and yet still hitting him, without mercy, for his own good. *Teach him a lesson.*

Then I imagined it a different way, where my Mom had the crowbar and I was at her feet, pleading. Dad was watching helplessly, like Silvia, terrified, but also happy that Mom was saving him from me.

All the faces kept spinning and changing, until there was no telling who was hitting, who was being hit, and who was being saved. I was all of them mixed together, the hand causing the pain, the face receiving it, and the horrified girl looking on. My father's voice was the soundtrack, the way he used to tease me, pretending to be blind, asking again and again, "Is that my Chlo?" I didn't want to hear him. I did not want to hear that voice. It must have been a hundred degrees in that boxcar.

★*★

Sometime in the afternoon, James asked me if he should give Clark his beer. The question jarred me out of my half sleep, making me realize how foolish it had been to let myself go, even a little. Luckily, Clark was still snoring. I said yes to the beer. Drinking might dull Clark's mind, the way it used to slow my Mom down. I needed every advantage.

James opened the first beer and put it in Clark's hand. Clark drank it without seeming to wake up. He jammed the neck of the bottle deep in his mouth, as if he wanted to bite it off. When he was done, he pulled it out like a pacifier and gasped. He sat up, but his eyes were still closed. James gave him another bottle. Clark drained it, too.

That opened his eyes. The only pause between bottles two and three was the time it took for Clark to peel off the sweaty labels, all the while staring at me as if he wished he was peeling off my skin. Then he wadded up the labels and threw them, one at a time, at James.

After three bottles, I said, "Enough." You wouldn't have believed the hatred Clark beamed at me when I said that.

I had hoped that the beer would slow Clark down, make him easier to deal with, but it had the opposite effect. Now he seemed super awake, his eyelids never closing, his reptilian eyes constantly tracking me.

Trains were coming and going, but ours was just sitting there, baking in the sun. By evening, I was going out of my mind. "Why aren't we *going?*" I said.

Silvia agreed. "Really, Finn," she said. "It's too tense."

Clark had been lying on his side, turned away from us. When he heard that, though, he sat up, folding his legs under himself like some kind of swami. After a final delicate dab at his cut, he put down his bloody newspaper as if it were a smoldering peace pipe. He turned to Silvia. "I apologize," he said. "For before. I hope we can still be friends."

I wanted to shout: liar! but Silvia was tired of all the silence. She looked exhausted. "We're going to California," she said. Clark nodded, then tried to hide the fact that nodding made him wince.

"Absolutely," he said. "That's excellent."

"Actually," I said, crossing eyes with Silvia, "it's not definite."

"But you *are* going west," Clark said.

"Maybe. Maybe not," I said.

For some reason, Silvia kept talking. "How long will that take?"

"What? To go west?" Clark said. "*West* is kind of vague."

"He's playing games with you," I said.

"Vague," Clark said, ignoring me, "because west's a direction, not a place. How long do you plan to rest here?" He was asking Silvia again, but I was sick of his questions.

"Until this goddamn train gets going," I said.

Clark's eyes widened, his nostrils flared, and then he doubled over, laughing silently. "Oh! Oh! That's rich!" he gasped.

"Shut up," I said.

"'Until this train gets going,'" Clark said, turning to James. "*Going!*" he wheezed.

James started to laugh, too, as if it was finally time to acknowledge the private joke between them. When I saw that, my heart sank.

"So?" I said.

"These cars are here for service," Clark said.

"They ain't going nowhere," James added.

I thought Clark would throw up, he was laughing so hard.

"What does he mean, *Nowhere?*" Silvia said. I wanted to shush her, but I didn't want Clark to show me up anymore, so instead I said, "It means we're on the wrong train."

"Bing bing bing bing bing!" Clark said.

"Say we *were* going to California," I said. "How long would that take?" Clark picked up his soiled newspaper and began folding it neatly in half, then in quarters, as if he wanted to save the business section for later. He liked making me wait for his answer. The fact that I wanted his opinion was restoring his confidence.

"You might be able to catch a coal train to Chicago," he said. "From there you could maybe ride out with the piggies on a nice hog train. Good weather? Say, two weeks."

"Two weeks!" Silvia said.

"Maybe less, if you had a decent guide," Clark said. I hated the sugary way he was talking to Silvia. I felt like saying the word "rape," just to remind everybody what I had saved her from.

"Well, that's out of the question," I said, but Silvia disagreed.

"It's not for you to decide, Chica," she said. She immediately added, "Finn."

"'Chica?'" Clark said. He stared at me for a long time, especially at my chest. "Isn't that a girl's name?"

"Mind your own damn business," I said. But he came nearer, squatting down and sniffing the air, as if he had just caught a whiff of the sheep under the wolf's clothing.

"Chica," he said. "Aw. That's sweet."

Just then I felt the crowbar slip away.

"I got it," James said, moving behind Clark. "Right here."

"Nice move," Clark said, taking the crowbar from James and smiling at me.

"Yeah, thanks a lot, James," I said.

James shrugged. "Man's gotta do what a man's gotta do," he said. He clapped his hands together, the way he did at the end of a routine.

It made a little cloud of chalk.

✦*✦

Clark had some fun with the crowbar for a while, pretending it was a sword, pointing it at my heart, lunging and saying "En garde!" like some kind of Musketeer. I was scared, but I was glad he was paying more attention to me than Silvia. I tried always to be in between them. It wasn't too hard. He seemed fascinated with me, now that I was a girl.

"We're going to have us a party tonight!" Clark said. He was sweating, and not just from the heat inside of the boxcar. The cut had made him feverish. His eyes went in and out of focus, and he forgot to wipe his wound, which was pouring out a clear yellow stream.

Dancing around with the crowbar, dripping with sweat, Clark looked like an Indian whooping it up in front of a bonfire. Silvia and I seemed to be his flames. He tried to take my arm to get me to dance with him, or at least spin around like a moron, which was what his dancing amounted to. Each time I pulled away from him, he thrust out his lower lip and said, "Cwark is vewy, vewy disappointed." But then he grabbed my arm and held the flat end of the crowbar—the sharp end—to my throat, hissing, "Dance with me."

I danced with him, close, right up next to the wound. When he saw me looking at it, he thrust his cheek at me, saying, "You like?" The gash smelled like fishy newspaper. He wiped his cheek with his fingertips and touched my forehead with them, blooding me, as if we were celebrating my first kill.

I was pretty dizzy after all that spinning around. Clark's hands were all over me, pinching and squeezing. My main thought was: *not in front of James*, even though he had betrayed me. I couldn't really see James. I couldn't see much of anything. The boxcar was almost dark.

The bonfire was only in my imagination. Clark leaned in. His face stank. "You're gonna be my special lady," he whispered. I felt his breath in my ear. Then his toothless gums were pinching my earlobe.

Silvia screamed "No!" from behind Clark's back. Suddenly, he was doubled over, and then he was on the ground, his hands jammed between his thighs. Silvia had kicked him right in the nads. She did it again when he was on the ground. His butt was up in the air. She just took aim and kicked him from behind. She must have hit home, because Clark started to throw up.

"Let's get out of here," she said. I stood over Clark, shaking. I still wanted to do something to him. The next thing I knew, I was crumpling up a twenty dollar bill and shoving it in his pukey mouth. I hoped he'd choke on it.

$$\star \, _\star ^\star$$

When Silvia and I were safely outside, I jammed the door with the crowbar. Silvia had second thoughts about that. "What if there's a fire?" she said. I said I hoped there would be, but then I remembered James, so I loosened the crowbar and told Silvia that they could get out in an emergency, even though I secretly doubted it. I could still hear Clark moaning and throwing up. It was sweet.

As it turns out, we didn't have to worry about James at all. We hadn't gone fifty feet when he suddenly appeared.

"Where'd you come from?" I said.

"The hatch," he said. "I fit right through."

I didn't say anything else to James. I was still mad at him for switching sides, but I didn't shoo him off, either. He followed Silvia and me out of the railroad yard, keeping a respectful distance. He understood he wasn't completely welcome.

We found a hole in the fence by the elevated highway. Before we climbed through, I stopped and took one last look at the train yard. From here, it was obvious that the California Pacific boxcars weren't going anywhere. They were set apart from the active tracks, all by themselves on a weed-choked stretch of rail.

We stopped for Silvia to catch her breath. She asked me why I had given Clark the money.

"Because my mouth was too dry to spit," I said.

chapter twenty

ylvia was breathing in shallow gulps like a goldfish, pressing her
fingers to her chest, as if her weak lungs needed some outside
help. I gave her some extra time to catch her breath. "Men are
pigs," I said.

Silvia shook her head. "Not all of them. You'll see."

"Shh. Don't talk. Just breathe," were the words I said, but what I
was really doing was apologizing for what I had put her through. After
everything that had happened, *she* was comforting *me!* She could be so
exasperating.

I pulled away from her when James walked up. He didn't have any
right to see Silvia and me being so close.

"What do *you* want?" I said.

"I know a place to crash," he said.

"I thought you lived on the trains."

"I was born here," he said. "This my city."

Silvia looked ready to collapse. I didn't have any better ideas, so
we fell in behind James. He made us wait while he found himself a
walking stick, a long piece of iron rod. He did a little pole vault with
it as a test. "Come on," he said. "It's a ways away."

James led us deep into the shadows under the elevated highway as
night fell. Silvia and I trudged behind him, trying to cheer each other
up, but the conversation always seemed to come back to men.

Even if it was an illusion, I felt safer under the highway. It was like walking under the belly of a long white beast asleep on its feet. The traffic overhead made a constant rough song, which I found soothing. Our path was as wide as a runway, with angled banks like a river. James called it a gutter. He said it was full of water after a big rain. A gutter was as good a name for it as any.

James looked so small and solemn with his walking stick, like a pygmy Moses. The iron stick rang out when it hit the ground. I stayed behind with Silvia, helping her along, letting her rest her cheek on my shoulder whenever she needed to. James was always ahead. He slowed down when we fell too far behind, but he was always pushing us to move on—not with words, but with impatient taps of his rod.

After—what, a mile? Who could tell when the concrete scenery was always identical?—but after a long time, we started passing cavernous metal pipes aimed downward at us from the banks like a firing squad. The first pipes were dry, but then we came across some that gave out a trickle of black water. Soon the puddles started. The farther we went, the larger they got, until there was so much water that we had to start walking on the angled banks. I learned how hard it is to walk at an angle. I could barely imagine what Silvia must have felt like, with the gravity working against her big belly.

We finally hit a flat stretch, which made it easier on the ankles but slowed us down on account of all the bunched-up rusted fences, the abandoned cars, and the rest of the dangerous junk we had to climb around. The water flowing under the highway had become a real stream, with rocks and eddies and a nice gurgle.

At a certain point, the stream became a full-blown river—sluggish, swollen with garbage, dotted with tires and dead fish, but a river, nonetheless. And all of it under the highway, matching it curve for curve. I'd been on that highway a million times and never known about the river below.

I asked James how much farther—more for Silvia's sake than mine. She was stopping every twenty yards to bend forward and rest her hands on her thighs. Her shoulders were drooping. She had a sour expression on her face, as if she'd been drinking from the brackish puddles. James didn't have anything to say. I started to worry that he had lied about being a native of this city. What if he was lost?

But he didn't walk like a lost person. He went in a more or less straight line, climbing on top of anything in the way, banging the roofs of torched cars with his staff, as if to drive out the ghosts of burnt drivers. Or he'd run along with a wheel-stuck grocery cart, coast a few feet before the cart tumbled, and jump clear of the wreck with a whoop, always landing on his feet.

Silvia was reaching her limit. James looked at her with disgust. He said there was a place up ahead to rest and get some water. Then he marched off at full speed and we lost sight of him for almost half an hour.

We would have walked right past him if he hadn't hissed at us— "Psst!"—and banged his staff. We were under an unlit section of highway, which meant that none of the usual foggy yellow light slanted down through the guardrails. It was almost pitch black. The river was high here. We were working our way along the busted-up foundation of some old brick building. I knew that because I kept bashing my toes into loose bricks. I walked ahead of Silvia, clearing the path like a soldier in a minefield.

James kept tapping, guiding us across the old foundation. There were tall weeds everywhere. Silvia found a tick on the back of my neck. She pinched it with her fingernails and flicked it away.

The air was fresher here. We were finally on higher ground than the expressway with its red and white streaming cars. There was a lovely splashing sound, but I was immediately skeptical, on account of all the filthy water we had seen that night. James was standing waist deep in a pool of frothy water, splashing around under—a *waterfall?*

"Come on in," he said. "Water's nice." I didn't go in just yet. First I helped Silvia lie down on an old stone wall next to the water, easing her through her long series of positions, from sitting to leaning sideways, to lowering herself on her side, to rolling on her back. Her eyes fell shut along the way, like a sleeping doll's. She made an involuntary grunt when her legs stretched out.

"That's good," she said, and in seconds she was snoring. I wasn't ready to get in the water yet, so I fussed with Silvia for a while, propping her head up off the stone with my shirt, her knees with my bunched-up pants. I dipped my hand in the water and brushed her forehead and cheeks with my fingers, as if I was painting sleep on her face. I did it more for me than for her, I suppose. It made a nice quiet moment.

Then I was ready. I took off everything else.

"Hey. You're naked," James said, but he didn't put much energy into teasing me, and I was certainly beyond caring.

"So call the President," I said, and got in the water. James moved out from under the waterfall so I could stand there for a while under its cleansing fists and just let it pound me. I didn't even care if the water was dirty, it felt so good.

When I was done, I moved off to the shallows, and sat there on a waterworn rock, enjoying the feeling of resting my palms on the wavy surface, as if my hands were waterbugs, the kind with the long skinny legs that never sink. It reminded me of a pool my father took me to one summer, when we lived in an oven of an apartment in the South. The pool itself was nothing—the usual bright blue hole—but I loved walking into the water on shallow rounded steps. There was a nice chrome handrail you could slide down, starting out above the water in the hot summer air and then slipping downwards, bit by bit, under the agitated surface. I used to play on those steps for hours. My father thought I was afraid of the deeper water. I let him think that, because it made him more attentive, but I actually liked playing on the steps much more than just swimming with the other kids.

Even here, with my butt on this bare rock, with the cold city water splashing down from above, so unlike that Southern pool, I liked the shallows, that nice feeling of half in, half out. Sitting there gave me a chance to look around. The crumbly walls of the ruin were all different stones, all irregular. They looked really old, but I wasn't sure. I didn't know anything about buildings, except what Miss Bellows had explained about the ancient Romans at the beginning of the year—how they knew how to cut stones and build everything with them. But the Romans never made it to America. I think the Americans just used whatever stones were lying around.

"What is this place?" I said.

"Meadow mill," James said. "It's old." He was sitting in the shallows, too, but keeping a distance. He didn't look at me, I guess out of respect for my being naked. I liked that. I felt clean and powerful again, and I wanted to talk to someone, even if it was James.

"How'd you find it?" I said.

"Aunt used to take me."

Silvia sighed and shifted on the wall. For a second, I thought she was going to roll off, but even sleeping people have a sense of limits. Her arm dangled over the edge, but that was it.

"Did you grow up around here?" I said. James pursed his lips. I could tell he didn't want to talk, but I didn't care.

"Aunt had me summers," he said.

"My father died when I was your age," I said. James suddenly got all tense.

"My father ain't dead. He just don't want me. Mother neither," he said.

"Sorry," I said. I had assumed his parents were dead.

"Ain't your fault," James said, dipping his head under the water. He came up with his cheeks full. He made a tiny "o" with his lips and spat an arched stream. "Pooty good," he said, when he was all out of water.

"Do you still have your tonsils?" I asked.

"Yeah. I got 'em."

"My Dad had his, too. He got a sore throat one time. His fever came and went, but it got too high at night. He wanted to go to the doctor. My Mom wouldn't let him. She said it cost too much."

"Sore throat? No big deal," James said.

"Yeah. By the time they took him to the hospital, the bacteria in his throat had got to his heart. He was in the hospital for a while. Then he died," I said. I hadn't said those words to anyone, ever, but they came easy here.

"Just like that?" James said. I nodded. "Damn," he said.

"But I got to say goodbye," I said. "Even if he didn't know it was me."

"There you go," James said. "That's something."

"It was stupid."

"What your Moms say? After."

I had to think about that. The whole funeral was a blur. So was the party afterwards, with everybody crammed into our apartment—how my grandmother had complained about the plastic cups and the white bread and the cold cuts, about their being cheap and low class, but everyone knew she wasn't talking about the food. That whole time, from the hospital to when we moved away, was only about two or three weeks, but I remember the feeling of living completely outside myself, having to be on constant display, and every night being so exhausted. Some nights I slept on the floor.

"I guess she sort of blames me," I said, but James's head was back underwater. I figured it was just as well. When James surfaced, I stayed quiet. I watched him be a fountain again. He didn't seem to mind that I never answered his question. He hadn't really wanted to talk in the first place.

✶* ✶

After a while longer in the water, we were both shivering. It was time to go. James was too embarrassed to take off his clothes to wring them out, so all he could do was bunch up the edges and squeeze them. I tried to wake Silvia up, but she didn't budge, so I just worked my clothes out from under her. I dried myself off with my pants, which wasn't very pleasant, but at least my shirt was mostly dry when I put it on. My super short hair dried in no time.

Things seemed more normal with my clothes on. I was suddenly annoyed with James for dragging us all over the city in the middle of the night.

"Where the hell are we going?" I demanded.

"It's close," James said. "Just chill." He went back down to the river. Silvia was still lying on the wall, groggy, wiping her eyes and saying, "Just leave me for a while, Chica. I have to get some rest." I pulled her up. She was sitting on the wall like Humpty Dumpty when James came back.

132

"I found a sweet ride," James said. We followed him down to the river. He had found an abandoned rowboat. I didn't care how bad it looked. The thought of not having to walk, of just drifting, was wonderful.

"I can't believe this piece of crap," I said, but we were already helping Silvia in, James on one side of her, me on the other. We put her on the wide seat towards the back of the boat. Then James and I pushed the boat mostly into the river. It left a big groove in the dirt.

I climbed in and sat on the floor in front of Silvia. James gave the boat a final shove and jumped in. It floated, but sat very low. Its edges were only a few inches above the water. "Are we sure about this?" I asked. James shrugged.

"She weighs a lot," he said.

"You're too nice," Silvia said. Apparently, she wasn't too sleepy to be sarcastic. I leaned back against her legs. She rubbed my head as if I was a good luck charm. "Quit it," I said, even though I liked the feel.

There weren't any oars, so James used his iron rod. He pushed us away from the bank. As soon as we got underway, a puddle formed in the bottom of the boat and soaked the seat of my pants. "This thing's leaking," I said. James acted as if it was no big deal, but Silvia got very anxious. I guessed she was thinking of her trip across the river into America, and the way those girls had disappeared.

"The water's only two foot deep," James said scornfully.

"How's the leak?" Silvia asked. I lied and said it had stopped.

It really was another world in that boat. Floating down the middle of the river gave me the feeling that nothing could touch us. The few gnarled trees on the banks reached out with their pathetic bare branches, as if they were begging for a ride. The river was its thickest here, at least a hundred feet wide, and cleaner, with lush weeds on either side. You could pretend it was the Amazon. Or the Mississippi.

James balanced himself on the front edge of the boat, curling his athletic toes around two metal cleats. I could tell he was really enjoying himself, steering us down the river, keeping a lookout. It was serious business, but every once in a while James would do something goofy, to keep us all on our toes. He liked pretending his pole was stuck in the ground and lifting himself into the air, hanging on to the pole and wiggling his legs while the boat almost left him behind. I liked his antics. Silvia hated them.

We floated down the river as if a wall of glass separated us from the world. The shore on either side of us was looking worse and worse. James warned us that we were going through a bad neighborhood. "They just as soon gut you as not," he said. I hoped that Silvia didn't know the verb "to gut." From the look on her face, she understood enough.

A stinking fog rose off the water. Through it, we could begin to see signs of human life. We drifted past makeshift tents that looked as if they had been spun by insects in the nook of trees. What I thought were tree stumps or piled tires, or just heaps of garbage, turned out, often as not, to be people sleeping on the ground. You couldn't tell if they were men or women. The junk they drew around themselves for warmth or camouflage made me think of hermit crabs.

At one bend in the river, where the ground dipped away sharply and there were little rolling whitecaps, James poled us over to shore. It was a mistake. A man rose up from the banks—looking more like a bear than a man, on account of the layers and layers of ragged clothes—screaming at us to "pay the toll." I thought he wanted money, and I fished in my pocket for some, but James said he was just a crazy preacher. "Money'll just encourage him," James said, knocking away a dead branch the preacher had thrown at us like a spear.

Then there was another bend, and suddenly the elevated highway veered off to the right, the river to the left. The orange sky opened up over us, and I realized how reassuring it had been to have the concrete all around us, and the constant thrum of motors and tires overhead. We were suddenly exposed. The banks of the river grew more wild and overgrown with tall grass, cattails, and mulberry trees. Anything could be hiding there, and the river was narrowing again. The rowboat was running aground all the time, the leak in the bottom getting bigger with each jolt. At a certain point, it became impossible for James to move us forward. Without any discussion, we abandoned ship. The water only came up to my shins.

It was eerie to be ankle deep in that water, with the wind ruffling the tall grass, and to see huge ugly brick apartment buildings, lying like beached battleships on the level plain, as if the little stream we had just left behind had once been a mile wide.

"It's the projects," James announced. Hearing him say that gave me a little thrill. I had heard about the projects in the news, mostly in terms of drugs or shootings or building implosions. But then, after we crawled and scratched our way onto dry land, James led us towards the huge buildings. He meant to take us inside one. The windows were dark, except for the blue flicker of televisions, as if we were in the middle of an air raid and people were tuned to the news.

"Your aunt lives *there?*" I said. James nodded.

"Hope so," he said. "Least she used to." James suddenly crouched down and started sifting through some trash, as if he had spotted a rare and delicious mushroom. It was hard to tell where the trash ended and the ground began. "Cash money," he said triumphantly, showing me his booty. It was a hypodermic needle, still fresh in its hospital wrapper.

chapter twenty-one

✳ ✳
✳
✳ ✳

The sight of the projects seemed to give James a boost. The closer we got to them, though, the farther back Silvia and I fell. Silvia kept telling me to just leave her behind, but it was appalling to picture her asleep on that open littered ground. James was too excited to wait up for us. In fact, he started jogging, and then, in the shadow of the building, he broke into a run.

Silvia and I picked our way through the broken glass and the mildewed mattresses, their foam spilling out like white guts. We climbed in slow motion through the barbed wire fence, which in most places wasn't even a fence, just a series of forlorn concrete posts, many of them broken. I stepped in a busted umbrella. Its pointy little ribs bit into my ankles like rats as I worked my feet free. I screamed "Get off!" The brick building seemed to magnify every sound and throw it back at us like an insult.

James waved to us from the entrance, a battered steel door set in a wall of pock-marked metal, as if a war had been fought here and the damage had been left to commemorate the battle. James held the door open for us. It was inconceivable to me that it wasn't locked.

The lobby—if you could call the rat maze from the front door to the elevator a "lobby"—felt like one of those check-cashing stores you see in bad neighborhoods, the kind with bulletproof glass everywhere. There was one like that near my Mom's house. The people who worked there always looked exhausted and scared, as if they constantly expected someone to stick them up.

The lobby stank of bacon grease and pee. James was by the elevator, pressing the "up" button every few seconds. It was already lit. I was mad at him for bringing us here. I felt like calling him an idiot for pressing a lit button. Silvia was sagging against me like a stack of firewood. The elevator was taking forever. I heard laughter outside, but I didn't want to believe it was people.

The front door flew open and slammed against its stop. A gang of boys burst into the lobby, as if the force of their laughter was a battering ram. I listened but I couldn't understand what they were saying, not even a single word. They treated the lobby like a locker room. They were celebrating. When they saw us, the noise stopped. Their faces went blank. They crossed their arms in front of their chests and fell into some kind of pecking order, like soldiers, with the leader out front, a massively muscled boy with two gold front teeth and a green plastic earring like a shower curtain ring. The other boys formed a wall behind him, their shoulders jammed together, their faces all frozen in a row like Mount Rushmore.

James stepped away from Silvia and me, and I thought: *You treacherous runt!* But actually he was standing between us and the boys, hardening his body into an aggressive little pose, just like them. He looked so puny. In my mind, I named the green earring boy "Goliath."

"Hello, hello," Goliath said. He was young enough that his voice hadn't completely changed. It amazed me that someone so young could be so in command. James didn't say anything. Silvia wanted to, but I squeezed her hand and kept her quiet.

"Check it out," Goliath said. "There's a baby soldier in our house." He came forward. The other boys didn't move. Their bodies just got more tense. Their gleaming sneakers flexed. "You bitches got something for me?" Goliath asked. He was talking over James now, to Silvia and me.

James didn't budge. "They with me," he said.

"They with *him*," said Goliath, over his shoulder. "The little man pimpin'." Then he laughed. The other boys waited a few seconds before joining in. They weren't sure when it was safe to start laughing. "Where you going, nigger?" he asked.

"Aunt house," James said. "Twelfth floor. Miss Officer Debbie."

The name startled one of the Rushmore boys. "Ain't she the one"— he said, but Goliath cut him off.

"You Miss *Officer* Debbie's family?" he asked. James nodded. Goliath put his hands on his hips, then broke out laughing again. "This little nigger Miss Officer Debbie's family!" Like magic, the tension broke. The boys started up with their wrestling and celebrating again, as if Silvia, James, and I had just vanished.

The elevator came. It was enormous, the size of two parking spaces. We all filed in. There were security cameras, but the lenses had been spray-painted black. Graffiti covered the walls: mysterious symbols, body parts, weapons. There were buttons for forty-two floors. James pushed twelve. One by one, the Rushmore boys pushed the buttons for their floors, which surprised me. I had assumed they all lived together in one big apartment.

The boys behaved themselves, shoving each other and cracking jokes, but staying apart from us. They didn't say goodbye when we got off on the twelfth floor, but there was an explosion of laughter when the elevator doors shut behind us. We burst out laughing, too, at least Silvia and I did, even though nothing was funny. James didn't laugh, but he smiled for the first time since I met him. "Miss *Officer* Debbie," I said, slapping the hallway's cinderblock walls. "That was perfect!"

"So what if she is?" James said.

"So what if she's *what?*" I said.

"Police. She works for the Man." He said this with pride, although it sounded like something from a TV show.

★ ★ ★

I didn't want to think about this. I was so tired of thinking about consequences! I had been leading Silvia around like a mule. I pulled her to a halt. "James," I said, "you're taking us to the police?"

"To my aunt house," he said.

"Who happens to be a cop."

"So what?" said James.

Silvia knew what it meant, too. She sank down to the sticky linoleum floor, put her hands over her ears, and started to cry.

"We can't stay there," I said.

"*You* can't. Don't mean *I* can't," James said.

"No, no, no, you should," I said. "Of course you should. It's just we can't."

"Let's just stay, Chica," Silvia said. "Please. I'm too tired."

"You want to stay?" I said. "Fine. Have a nice life in Mexico."

James shushed me. "People live here," he said.

Silvia was crying harder now, cradling her belly as if she were comforting a child. "I'm allowed to rest," she said. "I'm not a guilty person. I didn't do anything wrong."

We were stuck that way for a while. I didn't want to say anything because I knew it wouldn't come out right. I was pissed off, but I didn't really blame Silvia for being illegal. We just stood there in the hallway, frozen.

James was the one who finally got us unstuck. "I know a place you can sleep," he said. "I'll take you. But I'm coming back."

I thanked him and went to help Silvia up. She refused my hand. She took James's instead.

chapter twenty-two

✴ ✴ ✴
✴ ✴

Then it was down the massive elevator and back out into the night. Silvia refused my help, even when we went through the heavy front door. She preferred to let it hit her belly rather than have me hold it open for her. I couldn't really blame her for being mad. I felt like a coach who had refused to let one of her athletes quit a race. Part of me hoped she'd stay angry. I thought it might give her some extra strength.

The place James knew about was a park. He told us it wasn't too far away. Once we got out of the foul lobby and into the night air, which was heavy but still pretty fresh, I found I was less scared. Exhaustion wrapped itself around me like a blanket, weighing down my shoulders and tripping up my legs. Nothing could hurt me because nothing seemed real: not the scraggly bearded drunks asleep on the ground in their filthy stiff clothes; not the defiant sewer rats with their slicked-back hair; not the sidewalks shimmering with broken glass. I felt like a car with the windows rolled up.

We heard gunshots, but no sirens.

It was like walking through a bombed-out city, where the bombs had been dropped by stealthy American jets. There were gaping holes in the streets with weeds growing in them. The sidewalks were all broken and heaved up, but there were no tree roots to blame, no trees. I imagined furious men pounding the sidewalks with sledgehammers. Charcoal from old cooking fires moldered in the gutters. James saw me looking and said: *People live here.*

James waited for us at a mutilated stop sign. You could tell it was a stop sign from its shape, but the word "STOP" had been erased. All the paint had been blistered off, as if someone had tortured it with fire to shut it up. "Almost there," James said. I could tell he was looking forward to getting rid of us. He pointed down the street to a decrepit park lined with derelict townhouses. Silvia planted her feet when she saw it, as if she wanted to take root in the broken sidewalk.

"At least there are trees. Which is good," I said, but somewhere in the night I had lost my gift for lying.

"This was so stupid," Silvia said, but I couldn't tell which "this" she meant.

James took us into the park. It was as ruined, in its way, as the worst part of the river. The park was built on uneven ground. There were lots of rock outcroppings, perfect for climbing on if you were a kid, but from the adult look of the trash, this wasn't a playground, at least not for kids. "Quick. In here," James said. I didn't know what he was talking about until he was practically pushing me down in the dirt.

"Hey, take it easy," I said, but then I saw the hole, which was basically a shallow scooped-out cave under one of the biggest outcroppings.

"I'm not getting in there," said Silvia. "There could be animals."

Which meant that I had to get in first. I backed my way into the cave, kicking spastically every few inches, just in case. I felt around with my feet. "See," I said. "Piece of cake."

Silvia didn't fit at first, so James and I had to scoop out some more dirt. I couldn't do much. My wrist was starting to hurt again. I remembered what Dr. Locke had said at the hospital about losing my hand. After everything my wrist had been through, I was suddenly afraid of getting it dirty.

"You got a quarter?" James asked. At first I thought he wanted a tip, on account of his having to work so hard digging, but that turned out to be an insulting thing to think. I gave him one. He came back a few minutes later, his arms stacked to the chin with newspapers. "Make it a little nicer in there," he said, setting them down. The paper was still warm from the presses. The ink gave off a sharp smell, but a clean one, like shoe polish. It was better than the hole's general wet clay smell, which I associated with open graves. We spread out the news-papers and then Silvia and I settled in on top of them.

The newspapers helped, but the cave still felt like a roomy coffin. I lay back and tried not to look at the cobwebby slab, which was only a foot or so above our noses.

The last thing James did before he left was to pile up some junk in front of our cave, so that we could still see out, but other people couldn't see in. "Don't talk to nobody," James said, as if we were tod-dlers. I was really grateful to him, for everything, especially for talking with me back at the mill. "Can I give you some money?" I said. "Just to say thanks?" I tried to say it in the least insulting way possible, but money talk always ruins everything. James rose above it. He shook his head, and then, as a final salute, he did a handstand and walked away like that, balanced on his fingertips. "Be careful!" I said, thinking of all the glass on the ground. It was the last I saw of him.

★*★

You'd think that Silvia and I would have fallen asleep instantly, but we didn't. We didn't talk, either. We just slithered around like snakes for a while, trying to avoid lying on rocks. We were extra polite to each other, saying, "Excuse me," when our knees bumped. I wanted to apologize to Silvia a thousand times, but instead I was pulling away when my fingers brushed up against her cheek.

Then she was snoring, and I was left to face the night alone. I squirmed over to the edge of the cave and watched some rats forage, trying to imagine they were crabs. There was definitely an underwater feel to this place, as if the city was an ocean, and its whole crushing weight was resting on this park. A few homeless men drifted through the park like seahorses, stopping here or there to dig around in a wire trash can or laze on a bench for a while before drifting away. A gentle tide seemed to be moving them. I understood how it felt to try to set your own course but then to be pushed wherever by the invisible hand of the night.

I would have been happy to rest in my cave and think my gloomy thoughts, but I was distracted by the arrival of a small group of black people at the far end of the park. They were mostly men, but a few women, too, which surprised me. They were all dressed up, and talking and laughing politely, as if they had just come from church.

Two of the men stuck out—one because of his incredible height, the other because he was so handsome. Everybody treated the handsome one like a king. His head was shaved bald and he was wearing one of those fuzzy Kangol caps, which gave him an attractive exotic look. He was wearing a purple exercise suit, the kind that looks like it was made from a parachute, and spit-polished leather loafers. There was a huge gold ring on his left pinkie. He walked with a girl on each arm. I found the girls annoying. They were fawning all over him in their miniskirts and deep cleavage. I wondered why he put up with it.

The incredibly tall man was always by his side like a Secret Service man. It was the middle of the night and he was wearing sunglasses! His head scanned the park like a security camera. He was tall enough to be a basketball player, maybe seven feet, but that was judging from where I was, so low to the ground. He was wearing a pin-striped suit and an old-time hat, which made him look like an alien trying to blend in among earthlings.

The handsome one sat on the bench nearest to me, about twenty feet away. He was close enough for me to see that his ring was in the shape of a human skull, with rubies in the eye sockets. No one else sat down. They just kind of crowded around him. I heard someone call him "King D," and then, later, I heard him refer to himself that way. He talked about himself in the third person, like a politician. He kept saying "King D" *this* and "King D" *that.* It was like me walking around saying, "Chlo" *this,* "Chlo" *that.* But somehow it wasn't so strange coming from him. It made him sound more official.

It would go like this: King D would ask the tall man, "Who we got next, dog?" He said "dog" with affection, but I could tell it bothered his sidekick. Everyone else called the tall man "Lieutenant," or just "Tenant." Tenant would make a sign, waving his long elegant fingers, which, for some reason, made me think of a giraffe. Then a man or a woman would appear. The man's hat, if he had one, would be crumpled in his hands in front of his crotch. The woman would curtsy, or, if her skirt was too tight, maybe just bow. I finally figured it out: King D was a judge.

I couldn't hear most of what they were saying, but it was obvious that King D was settling complaints. He would listen, relaxing on the bench. His exercise suit made a high "wisp, wisp" sound when he shifted his legs. He looked like an old man feeding pigeons. At times, he would lean forward, nodding gravely, and say, "I hear you, player." He let the people speak until they were finished, even if what they were saying annoyed him, which it often did. At that point, he would raise his arms in the air, as if to say, "Enough!" and give his decision.

Almost everyone kneeled down and kissed his ring afterwards, even if the decision went against them.

Justice at his hands was so swift, the opposite of what I had seen in the courtroom with my grandparents. Everything there took forever. Most of the time, the judge couldn't do what he obviously wanted to because of some stupid technicality. Even if the judge did what he wanted, a lot of things fell through the cracks—the restraining order against my mother, for instance. I liked the way King D just listened, thought about the case for a minute, and decided.

*_**

Later that night, I saw something which changed my mind. King D had decided all the smaller cases. No one came forward when Tenant waved his giraffe fingers. King D looked tired. He got up to go, but Tenant whispered something in his ear. King D was shocked by the news. He started pacing. He rubbed his temples. He spat. He asked Tenant some questions. He told one of his bimbos to shut up. He told the other to bring him some mineral water. Then he nodded wearily and sat back down on his bench.

Tenant came back with a prisoner, a young man in a black hood. His hands were tied behind his back and he was barefoot. He walked delicately, as if his feet had eyes. Every few steps, he tried to clean off the soles of his feet, wiping them on his shins, but Tenant kept pushing him. The prisoner was brought in front of King D and made to kneel down.

King D began to ask him questions. He was very alert talking to the prisoner. Tenant kept a big hand wrapped around the man's neck, and shook him when it was time to answer. The questioning didn't take long. One time, the prisoner didn't answer, and Tenant punched him in the back of the head. After that, the prisoner was crying. I could tell because the hood was getting wet where it gathered at his chin.

King D sat for a while in silence. It was time for the verdict. King D didn't say it out loud. Instead, he silently made the shape of a gun with his thumb and fingers, held it up to the prisoner's hooded face, and pretended to pull the trigger. Tenant nodded and took the man away. From the way he struggled, he must have known what was in store.

✳ ✳ ✳

After that, I stopped watching. I crawled back to Silvia, who was sleeping sweetly, and lay my head on her belly. I needed to hear the baby's heartbeat. I felt like throwing up, but there was no food in me. I felt like digging down in the clay. I wanted my fingers to bleed from clawing at the ground. What right did King D have? Who did he think he was? Not even telling the man his sentence. No one deserved a trial like that, not even a monster. There was no law behind King D, except his own, and when I finally understood that, I knew I was in the wilderness.

chapter twenty-three

I probably would have slept through the night, all twisted up, my ear on Silvia's belly, if someone hadn't grabbed my ankle, shouting, "Don't tell me you done stole my stash!"

It turned out that James wasn't the only one who knew about our cave. Some insane drug dealer—another little boy, really—hauled me out of the cave by my leg. He started slapping me and demanding his stash. I told him I didn't know what he was talking about, and I really didn't. I had felt around in the cave. There wasn't anything in there except some beer cans and some other gross stuff, which Silvia and I tossed out when we put down the newspaper. I told the little drug dealer that, but he refused to listen.

That vicious punk might have hurt me if Tenant hadn't pulled him off, lifting him kicking and screaming way up in the air and then throwing him down on the ground like those wrestlers on TV, only this was for real. I started to thank Tenant, but he put a gigantic shoe on my chest and said, "Stay down."

We were brought before King D, and for a while I was still groggy and annoyed at being woken up and called a thief, so I was pretty rude. But then I remembered where I was.

King D asked me a bunch of questions, like what was I doing there and who was I working for. I told him I was just sleeping and minding my own business. The punk called me a skanky lying bitch, which I didn't exactly appreciate. King D told him to shut up. I was about to explain some more when Tenant called out from the mouth of the cave. "There's another one!" he cried.

"Show me," King D said. Tenant pulled Silvia out from under the rock. He dragged her over by her armpits. She was limp.

"She with you?" King D asked.

There was no point denying it. Now that Silvia was out in the open, there was no protecting her. Our fates were linked.

"This ain't no place for a white girl," King D said. "Middle of the night like this." He stared at Silvia, and *hmph*ed like a disappointed father. "Why ain't she up?" he asked. Silvia's arms were spread open because Tenant was squeezing her armpits so tight. The rest of her body was slack on the ground. Tenant took her jaw in his long fingers, tilted her head back, and answered. "She still asleep."

King D shook his head disapprovingly. "Woman was put on earth to take care of her babies," he said. The bimbos murmured in agreement. Then he looked at me. The moment of judgment was at hand. "What you seen tonight ain't none of your business," he said. "Maybe King D ought to tie you up, lay you down in the river. That what he should do?"

"No," I croaked, although part of me said *yes, please, just get it over with*.

"That'd get it for you, and for her," he said, nodding at Silvia. "But not the baby. Crime of the mother ain't no crime of the baby. Ain't that right."

"No," I said.

"No *what?*" King D snapped. "*No, that ain't right*, or No, King D, *you wrong?*"

He was confusing me with all the words. Every answer seemed to be "no," but that couldn't be right. Tears were running down my cheeks. I was so angry and humiliated. The bimbos were laughing at me. Their eyes seemed to say: *It's too late*. "You got everything right," I said weakly. "That's all I meant."

"Well, all right, then," King D said, relaxing back into the park bench. He lolled his head back. "Hear that?" he asked Tenant. "King D got everything right." Tenant's laugh sounded like someone blowing into a huge glass bottle. Then King D sat up on the very edge of the bench. His weight was up on his toes. His leg muscles rippled under the exercise suit. He rested his chin on his fist, flexing his forearm and frowning like that famous statue, The Thinker. He idly spun the pinkie ring with his thumb. The ruby-eyed skull looked like a jeweled planet, spinning in its tiny orbit around King D's pinkie. *Just like the rest of us*, I thought.

I imagined myself splashing down in the river, wrapped in plastic, the foul water seeping in, the rainbow fingers of the oil slicks on the surface closing over me like the folded hands of a mummy. King D stared right through me.

I was shivering. There was nothing to do. Everything was out of my hands now, like I was little again, and my whole existence rested on my father's words. For some reason, I remembered the time he took me up Sugarloaf Mountain. We drove as high up as we could. Then we left the car behind and walked to the top through a scraggly grove of pines. I complained the whole way. It was foggy. There was no view. I was thirsty. I had worn the wrong shoes and I had a big blister under my toe. I told him I hated this trip, but we just kept climbing. I couldn't see the top, not even when we reached it—the fog was just too thick. My father had to tell me we were there, that we couldn't get any higher. He sat us down on a rock and pulled roast beef sandwiches and bottles of lemonade out of my backpack, which I had made him carry from the car.

The picnic surprised me. I hadn't seen him pack it. He said: "There are more things in heaven and earth than are dreamt of in your little head." He said he was trying to quote Shakespeare. I told him it was a fairly condescending thing to say. We sat and waited for the fog to clear, and when it finally did, my teeth were chattering, even though he had his arm around me. The wind opened up a kingdom of green land and sunlit air. We saw fields and a silver river and mountains all the way to the horizon. "I wanted you to see your country," my father said, but what I saw was how happy it made him to show it to me.

I remembered all of that and it broke my heart. I had to swallow the word "Daddy." That's how much of a struggle it was not to cry.

King D sat back and fixed his yellow eyes on me. He said, "You still here?" as if he expected me to be gone.

He turned to Tenant. "Call them a cab," he said, matter-of-factly. Tenant let go of Silvia and pulled out a tiny cell phone. It looked ridiculous in his huge palm. He had to use the corner of a fingernail to dial it. He turned away when he started talking into it, as if he didn't want us to see him being polite.

Silvia was rubbing her eyes. "Chica, what's all this?" she asked me.

"Nothing," I said. "We're getting a cab."

chapter twenty-four

The name on the cab license said, "Ramanujan Punjab." Mr. Punjab was an old Sikh with a very clean white turban. His moustache was stained yellow in the middle from smoking a pipe. He was smoking it now. It made a wet sucking noise, as if he was drinking the smoke through a straw. The pipe smell gave the cab a nice homey feeling.

The cab's squeaky vinyl seat felt like civilization. "We're in," I said giddily, but Mr. Punjab didn't leave until Tenant tapped the hood. As we pulled away, he said, "Yes, boss," even though the windows were rolled up and Tenant couldn't possibly have heard him.

"Not a neighborhood for dilly-dallying," Mr. Punjab said. "Where am I taking you?"

"Two Hemlock Way," I said. It was Marion's address. Her house was the only place I could think of. I'd never been there, but I remembered the address because it sounded like old money. "It's in the suburbs," I added.

Mr. Punjab tapped his turban. "A complete map of the city resides in my brain," he said.

Mr. Punjab's cab had a digital readout for the speedometer—big green numbers. On narrow city streets I watched it climb to fifty-five, fifty-eight, and back down to three when we were stopped at a light. It never went down to zero, even when the car was standing still. Mr. Punjab noticed me looking at the speedometer. "The engine is thinking about going, even while at rest. A workaholic, this car." Then he laughed musically, which for some reason made me think of a goat.

We zoomed through the empty city. Mr. Punjab was a very good driver, so it felt safe and reckless at the same time. I was getting used to the idea of a nice long cab ride. The memory of the trip to Sugarloaf had sprung a leak, and now I couldn't stop remembering things about my father. It was torture, but also necessary, I suppose, like when a cowboy in the movies has to pull an arrow out of his bleeding leg. The memories kept coming, good and bad, but mostly good. I felt like a room filling up with water. It made me think of a dream I used to have of our house flooding, and me swimming through it, up and down the stairs, around the banister, floating five feet above the rugs, the water softer than my parents' Sunday morning bed, and not being afraid because for some reason I could still breathe—I had turned into a water creature.

Silvia lifted her head away from the window on her side of the cab. "Are you okay?" she asked.

"Just kind of tired," I said. She nodded and dozed off, saying, "It's been a long night."

I loved being in that cab, bouncing around on the backseat. I wasn't even afraid of what the ride was costing. *So what if it's a hundred dollars and I can't pay? I thought. What can Mr. Punjab do to me?*

I was ready to ride half the night—that's how far away I thought Marian's house must be from the projects. But the whole ride took less than fifteen minutes. The meter said we owed twelve dollars. Even Silvia, who always argued with cab drivers because she thought they were all thieves, thanked Mr. Punjab when he helped her out. He wouldn't accept my money. "That would be unheard of," he said, waving off the cash. "Your ride is a courtesy," he said. When I thanked him, he said, "No. Not me. You owe your gratitude to your benefactor, Mr. King D." He clucked his horn for us when he turned the corner. It was nice, the kind of thing the parents at the Field School did when they saw you walking home.

Marian's neighborhood was definitely rich. There were only one or two houses on a block. It felt as if we had landed on a peace-loving planet where armies no longer fought wars but spent their days gardening and mowing each other's lawns. Silvia relaxed a little. She said that someday she and Roberto might own a country villa. I didn't tell her that Marian's house was officially in the suburbs, not the country. My grandparents always made a big deal about Marian's family living in the suburbs, saying wasn't it a shame how some people had given up on the city. It was an empty complaint. There wasn't much difference between where my grandparents lived and the suburbs, at least not in the type of people who lived there. Everyone in both places was white.

Marian's house had enormous columns. Columns almost always look tacky, but Marian's house looked like it had earned its big columns. The lawn was incredible. It looked as though the house had fallen asleep and let a gauzy green blanket drop around its ankles. It was a beautiful house, but all I could think about was how selfish it was for just three people to live in it—not counting the servants.

I knew where to find Marian's window. She had described it to me enough times, telling me how I could throw bits of gravel from the driveway if I ever needed to "have a consultation" in the middle of the night. She claimed to be a light sleeper. I guess it was true, because as soon as the first handful of gravel hit her window, the light went on.

Instead of coming downstairs and opening the back door, Marian climbed out of the window and shimmied down the drainpipe, even though it ruined her nightgown. She didn't seem the least bit sleepy.

"Chlo!" she said, wiping a slimy clump of leaves off her sleeve. "How nice to see you! And you must be Silvia," she said, extending her hand and shaking Silvia's. "I've heard so much about you."

I wanted to tell her to stop sounding like her mother at a cocktail party, but I was too glad to see her. I asked her why she had climbed down the drainpipe instead of just coming downstairs. She said something about authenticity, which reminded me how strange she was. Then, like a fifty-year-old version of herself, she said, "But where are my manners?" She took us deep into the backyard to what she called the "gardening shed," but which was actually an entire little house. "It's not Buckingham Palace," she said. "I hope it'll do." She harshed on it the way people do when they're actually very proud of something. Truth was, it really did look like Buckingham Palace to me, and probably to Silvia, too.

The "shed" was full of very fancy lighting. "I'll be right back with a snack," Marian said, flicking on rows and rows of light switches. "Make yourselves at home." I couldn't believe that such a nice place was empty most of the time. There were Oriental rugs and antiques everywhere. Silvia patted the leather cushions on the sofa. "First class," she said, plopping down with an *oomph*.

Marian was taking forever. I hate to admit it, but I began to doubt her. I tried to imagine what I'd do in her place. One of the things I imagined I'd do would be to wake up my parents—assuming I was Marian and I lived with my parents instead of my grandparents—and tell them to call an ambulance right away for Silvia. I could see the logic of that, but I was worried because that plan didn't take into consideration the fact that Silvia was illegal, not to mention wanted by the police for kidnapping and blowing up a nice house in the city.

I shouldn't have worried. After all, Marian was Marian. It never would have crossed her mind to do anything as simple and direct as waking up her parents and calling an ambulance. She came back with a big bowl of salad and some crackers and cheese, kicking her shoes off in the front hallway and leaving them where they fell. She sat across from us at the marble-topped dining room table watching Silvia dig into the salad. I was starving, but I let Silvia get a good head start.

Marian made us tell her everything that had happened, in detail. I didn't like the expression on her face for most of it, which was feverish and fascinated, as if we were just some characters in a story, and not actual people who had dealt with so much. She kept whispering, "You poor dears," but she was obviously jealous of what we had been through.

When she asked, "What are you going to do now?" I realized that I had run out of ideas. The week's turmoil, the pain in my wrist, worrying about Silvia and the baby—all of it had just about done me in, so when Marian suggested that she and I go to the "lodge"—that's what she called the main house—and work on a plan, I said *fine*. We made up a bed for Silvia on the couch and buried her under a heap of incredibly soft blankets. She was asleep in no time, which helped me feel I wasn't abandoning her, just changing locales.

Marian probably would have made me climb up into her room if it hadn't been for my wrist. She offered to help me up the drainpipe if I thought it was "important for consistency's sake," but I told her she was crazy and to just let me in the back door like a normal person.

The lodge was incredibly clean. Everything smelled either like furniture polish or gourmet food. Marian sat me down at the kitchen table and made me a milkshake, which tasted fantastic. I worried that the noise from the milkshake maker would wake her parents up, but she told me that was silly because there were at least five closed doors between us and them.

Marian watched with greedy eyes as I drank the shake, as if she had laced it with truth serum. I called her on it. She said she was sorry. She was just so impressed with all I had done with Silvia. The way she said it was all wrong, as if Silvia were a prize show dog. I said that I hadn't really done much of anything for Silvia, except to get her kicked out of a good hospital for supposedly kidnapping me.

Marian got to talking about what had been going on at the Field School in my absence. It was a relief to hear about the normal world. The spotless kitchen and the milkshake and the gossip were all so nice that I stopped thinking about Silvia altogether for a while. Marian finally said that she had to go upstairs and get ready for school. It was already seven thirty in the morning. I panicked about her parents, but she said they always slept in. Even on weekdays.

Marian told me to get some sleep. She said there was plenty of room for me at the lodge. I told her to forget it, a little sharply, probably, because I didn't want to admit to myself how attractive an idea it was. I said that I had to look out for Silvia and that I still had no idea what to do with her. Marian laughed.

"You're going to fly her to California, silly. We can't let geography stand in the way of True Love." I told her to quit joking, but she went and got her little purse and pulled out a VISA card with her own name on it. Then she called up an airline and made two reservations on a flight to California.

After she hung up, she talked to me like a travel agent. "Your flight leaves in a few hours," she said. "They wouldn't let me buy the tickets over the phone. It's too last-minute. You'll have to take my card with you."

She wouldn't tell me how much the tickets cost. I had some idea, though. Once, when I was little, I called to find out how much it would cost to fly away from my mother's house that same day. The price the airline quoted me was astronomical. The airline lady told me that most tickets were bought far in advance. Only business people and the very wealthy bought tickets the same day they were flying.

Marian yawned and said that I wasn't seeing the Forest for the Trees. She packed me off to the gardening shed with some roast chicken and a bagel. As I stumbled through the wet morning grass, I thought about how money made certain things so much easier. I was grateful to Marian, which annoyed me, because she had given me so many new reasons to really dislike her.

chapter twenty-five

✳   ✳   ✳
✳   ✳

ilvia couldn't believe that we were really going to California.
"It's so wonderful!" she said. "Roberto will see his baby
being born." I told her to calm down because we weren't there
yet, but I was actually getting excited, too.

Marian came back to the shed to say goodbye. She made me practice her signature a few times. She said that sometimes they checked
the signature when a young person made a big purchase. Then she
kissed Silvia on the cheeks and slipped me a wad of cash, saying, "God
speed!", as if we were about to board the Titanic. I didn't count the
money until after she left. Somehow, she had managed to scrape
together almost two hundred dollars.

Silvia was against taking a cab, because she wanted to have some
money left when we got to L.A., but I was in charge of the money. I
knew for a fact that we wouldn't find any public transportation to the
airport, at least not around here, where everybody had a car. It was
even harder to find a cab than I thought it would be. When we finally
managed to flag one down, the cabbie kept telling us how lucky we
were because cabs almost never came out to Marian's neighborhood.
"Out here," he said, "mainly you got your limos."

All during the ride to the airport, Silvia talked about Roberto and
the life that they would make in L.A. It was good to see her so happy.
I let her go on and on about it, wondering where I fit in her plan. I
started thinking about a new life in California for myself, but for some

reason I couldn't picture it. I wondered what was holding me back.

The cab ride cost twenty-two dollars. When I paid, the cabbie looked over his shoulder and said, "No luggage?" as if he was noticing for the first time. "Just what you see," I said. It took both of us to pull Silvia out of the back seat.

All that was left was to buy the tickets. When we got up to the counter, a chubby airline man with a high voice and moussed hair asked me if "the lady," meaning Silvia, would be flying with me. I said yes, of course. The airline man said he was very sorry but he wouldn't be able to sell me a ticket for her, at least not for a flight today. I could see he was serious, so I did what my grandmother would have done. I made a big show of studying his name tag. I used his first name—Patrick—when I asked to see his manager. Patrick said he was the manager. Then I got angry. I said it was *deplorable*—I actually used that word—the way his airline treated Mexicans. I said it loud enough for the other people in line to hear.

Patrick got all embarrassed. He made a general announcement to the people in line: his airline didn't discriminate on the basis of race, creed, or color. The problem, he said, turning back to me, was how pregnant Silvia was. "So you're saying that the airline discriminates against pregnant people?" I said triumphantly. The people in line laughed quietly and started to mind their own business. Then Patrick got very snotty. He explained that it was the airline's policy not to fly a very pregnant woman. What if the baby decided to be born in the middle of the flight? That would be dangerous for the lady and her baby, and extremely inconvenient for the other passengers, now wouldn't it?

I was all out of answers. I took Silvia away and sat her down on one of the plush leather and chrome airport benches. I told her we wouldn't be going to California after all.

You can imagine how she took the news. For once, I was glad of the noise of planes. Anything was better than Silvia's sobbing. Usually I'm embarrassed by people crying in public, but Silvia had an impeccable reason. I tried my best to shield her from all the curious travelers. My grandfather says it's human nature to be curious about other people's tragedies. Of course, he's not exactly the most compassionate man on the planet.

Suddenly, something warm seeped under my leg. Silvia doubled over and gave a low moan and said she couldn't hold the baby inside any longer. Her water had broken, for real this time!

I screamed "Call an ambulance!" but people just stood by as if Silvia and I were a TV show. I kept screaming. Finally, Patrick came over with some paramedics and two policemen. They came running up with a gurney and rolled Silvia onto it.

I held Silvia's hand and told her she was doing fine, even though she looked pale and was shivering. She kept saying, "Call Roberto." I told her I didn't have his telephone number. Every time she tried to tell me, the paramedics pushed me away. From the look on their faces, I could tell that something was wrong. One of the policemen, a tall one with a walrus mustache, asked me to please step aside, but I kept coming back. I had to get Roberto's number.

The policeman grabbed me by the shoulder, but I pulled away. They were wheeling Silvia down a long glass corridor and I was running along with them. Silvia was writhing on the gurney and the paramedics were saying tense things to each other about her condition, which was apparently deteriorating. They were shouting at people to get out of the way. Outside, airplanes took off and landed as if nothing was happening. A luggage train down on the tarmac was keeping pace with us. We all seemed to be accelerating. The emergency was pushing us forward like a cannonball.

At least that's the feeling I had until the walrus policeman took me by the wrist—the bad one—and yanked it behind my back.

chapter twenty-six

They say you don't remember surgery, but I remember plenty about mine, including some of the things leading up to it. I remember waking up in the ambulance and looking over and seeing Silvia. She looked awful. Her face was puffy and there was an oxygen mask over her mouth. Tubes and needles were jammed in all over her body. A doctor was giving the paramedics instructions over the radio. The walrus policeman was crouching awkwardly between me and Silvia, his gangly arms and legs constantly getting in the way. The paramedics were silently annoyed with him. The policeman was apologizing for just doing his job. I remember wondering what his job was, exactly, and then I was out again.

I remember the ceiling tiles in the hospital hallway. A lot of them were stained, as if someone had spilled coffee on them. In my drugged state, I got to thinking that the ceiling was the floor of a cafeteria. It made me wonder what were we doing upside down, rolling across the ceiling. I tried to say something about it, but someone had cut the wire connecting my tongue to my brain.

I remembered a series of distant pops, which at the time I thought were gunshots, but which they told me later was probably the I.V. needle going in. They said they had to try several times before they found my vein. The sound reminded me of King D and the hooded man. I must have said, "Call the police!", because a nurse told me the police were already there.

And then I was in a bed with cold sheets, the kind that are so stiff they seem more like cardboard than fabric. The TV was on. The people on TV were laughing and laughing. My room had a window. I was surprised to see that it was dark the next time I looked out. A nurse stuck her head in the door and said that my parents were here and that she would send them in after the doctor had a chance to fill them in on my surgery—which, by the way, had gone really, really well, she added.

Her shower-capped head disappeared again, and the room was dark except for the TV, and suddenly I was full of anxiety, because I thought that Bobby and my mother had somehow figured out where I was. The nurse had definitely said "parents."

A handsome couple in evening clothes stuck their worried heads in the door. They looked at me, and then at each other, in confusion. Before disappearing, they apologized for bothering me. The woman looked familiar, but I couldn't place her. Still, I was relieved. Anybody was better than my mother.

Then the handsome couple reappeared, this time with the doctor, whose wild gray eyebrows I suddenly remembered from the operating room. At some point, I guess right at the beginning of the surgery, I had seen him, and imagined that I was being operated on by an owl who was replacing my hand with a wing, which I found both funny and deeply disturbing.

But now he just looked like a doctor. He acted like one, too. He asked me how I was doing without even looking at me. Then he picked up the chart at the end of the bed, turned to the couple, and said, "According to this, Marian's doing fine." The man and woman looked at each other, then at me, and at each other again. The woman nudged the man, who finally cleared his throat and said, "Doctor, there must be some mistake. This isn't Marian." The doctor looked at the chart again and said, "Are you sure? According to this, her name is Marian Williams." The woman said she thought she was qualified to identify her own daughter.

It was Marian's mother! I had seen her once or twice at Field, but always through tinted glass.

The doctor apologized and called in the nurse, who was very embarrassed. The nurse defended herself by saying that the only identification I had had on me was a credit card. She had called up the credit card company, read them the name on the card, and they had released the parents' work numbers.

I didn't want to get Marian in trouble, so I finally introduced myself. I said I was a classmate of Marian's, and that she had lent me the card. Marian's father, who was handsome but very stiff, started to lecture me about how inappropriate it was to borrow a credit card. He said he was quite sure that Marian knew better—implying that I had weaseled the card out of her! That's how well Mr. Williams knew his daughter.

Then the doctor did a very doctorly thing. He asked Marian's father to please remember that I was a patient and that the first thing I needed was rest. He herded Marian's parents out of the room and closed the door quietly behind himself, but not before giving me a friendly—if patronizing—wink.

I was almost asleep when it finally occurred to me to ask whether Silvia had had a boy or a girl.

chapter twenty-seven

I woke up to the sound of my grandfather clearing his throat. My grandmother had pulled a chair up next to the bed. She was fussing with my bedsheet, folding and flattening it, as if the edge of her little hand was a hot iron. My grandfather was over by the window, fiddling with the air conditioning. My wrist was throbbing, but I didn't mind the pain so much. The nurse had warned me. Besides, now I knew I was healing.

My grandmother pulled herself together and made a sort of speechy announcement, which was punctuated by my grandfather's throat-clearing. She said they both had missed me terribly and hoped I could put behind me whatever anger I had about the "situation with the girl." She said she wanted us to be a family again. Then she paused and stared at my grandfather until he said, "Needless to say, that goes for both of us."

I said something noncommittal, like "We'll see." I knew my grandmother would take that as a "yes" to being a family, but, in my mind, the matter was far from settled. I asked about Silvia. You'd have thought she was dead from the way my grandparents looked at each other. My grandmother said that there was a police officer outside who wanted to talk to me about that. The fact that my grandmother couldn't just come out and say things was a disappointment. I was learning a lot about her limits as a person.

On their way out, they sent in the policeman. I was all set to take a hostile attitude on Silvia's behalf, when who should walk in but the cop from the Krispy Kreme! He said, "Remember me?"

And I said, "Of course I do. You're the jerk who didn't believe me." He laughed. He told me he was sorry about that, but one of the first rules of dealing with kidnappers was not to surprise them, at least not when they can harm the parcel. I liked the sound of that, being called the "parcel." I imagined myself wrapped in brown paper and stamped "fragile."

He introduced himself as Officer Josh and told me that he had taken me very seriously that night. He had written down the license plate number of Bobby's van. Later on, he had put everything together —the report of a girl matching my description being kidnapped; the explosion at my grandparents' house; descriptions of an airbrushed van from my grandparents' neighbors. He said that finding Bobby and my mother had been pretty easy, but they were refusing to talk. The police needed my help with the kidnapping charge.

Essentially, Officer Josh was asking me to rat out my mother. I was still furious at her, but I wasn't sure I could sit in a courtroom and testify with her staring at me.

Officer Josh said that he understood it would be a difficult decision for me to make and that I could take some time to think about it. He said that there was still some confusion about what had happened. For instance, there was the involvement of the illegal alien to clear up. Some of his colleagues thought she might have been involved, both in the kidnapping and the explosion. I scoffed at that. Silvia was the most innocent person in the world, and I told him so. He asked me for my account of the kidnapping and the business at my grandparents' house. I told him everything.

When I finished, he whistled and said I sounded like a very resourceful person. He asked me to please not be offended by the question, but was I making anything up to protect Silvia? I said, "I swear to God," and for once, I had the feeling I was telling the truth as convincingly as I told the very best lie.

***

I got a chance to see Silvia later that day. Josh—I abandoned the "Officer" part fairly quickly—brought in a wheelchair and rolled me to a different part of the hospital. It wasn't the maternity department. I think it was some kind of psychiatric ward. You had to be buzzed in by a security guard. The doors were all bolted from the outside. A policeman sat in a folding chair at the end of the hall, reading a magazine and sipping a cup of coffee through one of those tiny straws. He snapped to attention when he saw Josh and said that there wasn't a whole lot to report. Josh asked if we could go in. He was just asking to be courteous. The other policeman was obviously below him in rank.

I asked if I could see Silvia alone and Josh said he was sorry, but no. He stood in the doorway and told me to go in. I was reluctant to, until he promised not to eavesdrop. In movies a lot of times, conversations that people think are private get used against them at trial. Josh seemed to know what I was thinking. He put his hands over his ears like a "Hear no evil" monkey and said, "Go on in."

I shouldn't have been paranoid about being overheard. Silvia and I barely spoke. She was lying with her back to the door. Her hair was a mess. It upset me that the room was stale. Silvia was a fanatic for fresh air. I didn't even bother to try the window. It was welded shut.

I sat down on the edge of the bed, trying to find a natural place to put my arm with its clunky cast, but I couldn't get comfortable. I didn't talk right away. I pulled Silvia's hair out of her face and hooked it behind her ear. Her pillow was soaking wet. It smelled sour.

She was silent, even after I asked her how she was doing. She looked at me out of the corner of her eye like a wounded animal, as if I was the hunter that had just shot her. I hated seeing her like that as much as she hated being seen. I kept trying to convince myself that she appreciated my being there.

I sat with Silvia for about ten minutes before Josh cleared his throat and said it was time to leave Ms. Morales alone. I told her I was sure they'd let her see her baby soon, but I doubted it was true. My lie was strictly amateur hour.

I couldn't wait to be out of that ward with its buzzing locks. When we were out in a brighter hallway, I asked Josh if Silvia's baby had died. I could tell he was a little startled by the question, but he was used to telling people hard things. He told me that Silvia had given birth to a very healthy baby girl, but that the policy in criminal cases was to separate the mother and the baby at birth, for the welfare of the child.

I made Josh take me to see Silvia's baby. She was very tiny and beautiful, wrapped up like a white cigar in her baby blanket. The name on the crib said "Baby Morales." I asked a nurse why Silvia's baby didn't have a first name like all the other babies. She told me that Silvia had named the baby "Chloe," but in cases like this, the mother's wishes weren't generally taken into account.

chapter twenty-eight

*   *
      *
  *   *

$\int$eeing baby Morales clinched it. On the way back to my room, I told Josh I'd be willing to testify against my mother. Josh said he appreciated that, but there was also the matter of Silvia's being an illegal alien. He said that even if she were cleared of all the charges against her, she'd still be sent home to Mexico. I said that was okay, as long as she got to take her baby with her. Josh said, "Of course," and I believed him. "Hey, look," he said, bumping my door open with the wheelchair. "You've got a visitor."

It was Marian. She was wearing all black, including a black beret. I asked her if someone had died and she said no, that she was wearing black in honor of Silvia's tragic circumstances, as a sign of respect. The more I learned about the world, the less Marian amused me. I told her that Silvia didn't need people wearing black. What she needed was help staying in the country.

"Oh, really?" Marian asked, in a kind of drawl, the kind she uses when she has something up her sleeve. She wouldn't answer any of my questions. She said she needed to see Silvia before she'd explain herself.

I took Marian over to the psychiatric ward—which is where *she* really belonged—but they didn't let us in, even after Marian pretended to be from the Mexican embassy. Marian's Mexican accent sounded like a taco commercial, but even a perfect accent wouldn't have worked. The Mexican embassy had just called to say that Silvia's case was a matter for the police and that she would have to deal with it on her own.

I tried to take Marian to see Baby Morales, but there was a new nurse at the desk and they wouldn't let us in because we weren't family. I didn't tell Marian about the baby's name. That's just the kind of information she would have abused.

We had struck out. Even the cafeteria was closed for construction. We wound up in the lobby, sliding around on hard plastic chairs. Marian pretended to be interested in my cast for a while, but she kept looking towards the hospital entrance. I asked if she had someplace better to be.

"Whatever gives you that impression?" she said. Her haughtiness only confirmed my suspicions.

Then, of all the people in the world, Roberto walked in. His gold teeth flashed in the flourescent light. He stopped in front of the Information Desk, looking anxious and lost.

"I have a confession to make," Marian blurted. "I made a few calls."

Roberto saw us and came over and gave me a huge hug, which he had never done before but which under the circumstances was perfectly appropriate. He thanked me for all I had done for Silvia, which stung a little. I introduced Roberto to Marian, and even though he was extremely keen to see Silvia, he thanked her and kissed Marian's hand—not in a goofy way, but in a very natural way. I wanted to know what was up with that, but Marian just smiled and made a big "Okay" sign with her fingers behind his back.

Roberto wanted to see Silvia right away. I explained on the way over that she was being guarded by police and that he could try, but I was pretty sure they wouldn't let him in. I had never seen him so determined. It made him very handsome.

When we got to Silvia's ward, the guard stopped him at the desk and asked him what his business was. He said he was Silvia's husband and he demanded to see her right away. The guard was impressed. He immediately picked up a telephone and spoke quietly into it. He made out a special pass for Roberto and said that "the children"—meaning Marian and me—would have to wait outside.

While we were waiting, Marian told me that she had gotten Roberto's number from Silvia, back when we were in the gardening shed. She had done it secretly, so I wouldn't think she was butting in. "Butting into what?" I said.

"Your adventure," she said. "Hell-o?"

Then Marian told me she had called VISA to make sure the charge for the airplane tickets had gone through. They told her it hadn't, so she called the airline. Her next call was to Roberto, telling him to come right away. She didn't mention it, but I was sure she bought Roberto's ticket.

I told Marian she was awesome, but secretly I was furious that the one thing she had done for Silvia was better than everything I had done for her, put together.

I changed the subject. I said I couldn't believe what a smart move it was for Roberto to say he was Silvia's husband. That made him family, which was the one category of person they said was allowed to see Silvia. The baby didn't count as family, apparently. Marian said she thought Roberto was a perfect gentleman, and understood why Silvia had Surrendered Her Sacred Prize for a guy like that.

Roberto came out about fifteen minutes later. His hands were shaking. I made him sit down and catch his breath.

"She looks awful," he said. "Just terrible."

I told him that having babies takes a serious toll on women and that they often looked the worse for wear. I didn't know it for a fact, but it sounded like common sense. I asked Roberto if he wanted to see his baby. "My baby?" he said. The words surprised him. "Of course I do. But not before Silvia's turn."

Then we just sat there, listening to the announcements over the P.A. Marian got up to make a phone call, which left me alone with Roberto. I thought of asking him about his trip and how things were going in L.A., but it just seemed too trivial, so I told him what had happened at the airport when Silvia and I tried to fly out to see him.

"Marian told me the same thing," he said. "I'm glad Silvia didn't have the baby on the plane. So maybe it was very lucky."

I didn't know what else to say, so I told Roberto how impressed I was with his lie about being Silvia's husband.

"It's no lie," he said, rubbing the corners of his eyes with his thumbs. "Silvia is my lawful wife."

I was dumbstruck. "But she told me you were just her boyfriend," I said.

"I made her do that. Our marriage is a secret. My parents don't approve."

Roberto told me he still lived with his parents. His visits to Silvia were as much a secret to them as to my grandparents. It was too bad Marian wasn't there. This Romeo and Juliet business was the kind of thing she ate for breakfast.

"So the baby isn't..."

"No," Roberto said. "She is legitimate." He seemed grateful that I hadn't said it the other way.

"And Silvia's here legally? I mean in this country?"

"Well, mostly," he said. "We made her application, as my wife.

Her papers are in order. At least they were, before all the trouble. Now, with this, I could lose my own visa."

"But you didn't do anything wrong!" I said.

"Of course not. But that's not the point."

Roberto told me that one of his friends had gotten sent back to Mexico for not having his car inspected in time.

I wanted to tell him how unfair everything was, but I couldn't think of a good way to say it, so instead I rubbed his back and said, "We'll work it out."

He nodded and said, "Sure, sure."

Marian finally appeared. I could tell she wanted to help cheer Roberto up, but for once she left well enough alone.

chapter twenty-nine

Finally, it was my turn to have a good idea.

I left Roberto in Marian's hands and called my grandparents. They were staying at the Colonial, a fancy downtown hotel, while their house was being fixed. My grandmother answered the phone, as usual. I asked her to get my grandfather on the line. She said he was "indisposed," which was code for his being in the bathroom, but I said I'd wait. There was a long, difficult silence.

When my grandfather finally picked up, I told him that Roberto and Silvia were married and that Silvia wasn't illegal after all. I said I'd be willing to be a family again if my grandfather called his friend the judge—the one who gave them custody of me—and asked him to straighten everything out with the police.

My grandfather agreed to my terms. There was a pause, and I could tell he was about to say something obnoxious. My grandmother sensed it, too. She said, "Eskimo, Herbert."

It was strange to hear her say that. I had forgotten his name was Herbert.

★*★

The judge fixed things in less than an hour. Silvia was moved to a normal room, a completely private one where she could have visitors. I was there when they introduced her to her daughter. The baby almost drowned in Silvia's snotty tears. The nurses actually had to threaten to take little Chloe away if Silvia didn't calm down. Roberto was filling up the windowsill with stuffed animals and disappearing every five minutes to buy a new disposable camera.

My grandparents came by that afternoon. My grandfather brought little Chloe a stuffed donkey. My grandmother was on her best behavior, giving Silvia advice about diapers which was about fifty years obsolete. Then she snapped open her purse and pulled out a thick envelope. "This is something for you," she said, handing it to Silvia.

Silvia opened it up. She started to cry when she saw how much money was inside. She showed it to Roberto, who was shaking his head even before he looked.

"We can't accept this," he said. "Really, there's no need. We're fine."

My grandmother took the envelope from him and gave it back to Silvia. "It's not for you, Roberto. It's for the baby's education."

Silvia still didn't want to accept it. I wouldn't have blamed her for holding a grudge against my grandparents, after the way they treated her, but that wasn't it. Silvia was just embarrassed by the size of the gift. My grandmother had to be sneaky.

"Think of it as back wages," she said, which did the trick.

★*★

I tried not to be a sap when it came time to say goodbye. I told Silvia I thought she was an amazing individual and I wished her good luck in California. I couldn't think of any words for how I really felt. All that came to mind were clichés. Silvia told me she thought of me as her little sister. She said she'd remember me every time she wrote her daughter's name. We hugged. She cleaned off my shoulder with some Kleenex. I tickled little Chloe's nose one last time. Then I said,

176

"Look at this gorgeous family," and it was time for me to go.

✦ ✦ ✦

After the goodbye, I went back to the hotel with my grandparents in their fancy car. The police still had the Dodge.

My grandparents didn't talk to me. They just let me cry, which I appreciated.

When I was feeling a little better, I asked if we could visit my father's grave sometime. My grandparents looked at each other. It took a minute for my grandmother to compose herself. She broke out some Wet-Naps from the glove compartment. She passed one back to me, saying, "Of course we can." She didn't try to comfort me beyond that. She didn't have any right to—at least not yet—and she knew it.

We were on the freeway for a long time before I realized we were driving above the river. What a different world at highway speed! The river was invisible. I could barely remember how it smelled. I opened my window, but the car was too full of my grandmother's perfume. A sign flew by, one of those historical markers. The name of the river was on it, in tiny words I could barely read. The river had an Indian name, with lots of "o"s and "c"s and "q"s. I wanted to know how to pronounce it. It was the kind of thing my grandfather knew, but I didn't ask him.

✦ ✦ ✦

When we pulled into the driveway in front of the Colonial, a black man in white gloves and a silk top hat opened the door for me. He smiled at me like a robot. I said "Thank you," like a robot. It seemed perfectly normal at the time. I was sealed up in the hotel's revolving door before it occurred to me that elevator men weren't really extinct. It's amazing how quickly you fall back on unthinking habits.

The lobby felt unthinking, too, with its artificial flowers and muzak and ritzy furniture. All the guests were white. So were the people behind the counter. There were two black men, but they were wearing tight hotel uniforms which blended in with the wallpaper. They looked uncomfortable and bored. They smiled when they realized I was looking at them. My grandmother said, "Isn't this a nice place?"

"Sure," I said, "if you're into apartheid."

My grandfather's face soured. "This is a first class hotel," he said.

My grandmother took his arm. "I thought we were all going to try," she said.

They showed me my room, which had an automatic lock on the front door. It opened with a white credit card. Their room was connected to mine by an inside door. They showed me the swimming pool up on the roof, which had an unbelievable view of the city. I stood for a few minutes at the edge of the roof, leaning against the guard rail and watching the night traffic. *Finally,* I thought, *something to show Marian.*

Looking out on the city, I thought about James. I wondered if he was safe at his aunt's house. I couldn't seem to find the projects. I went all around the roof, but never saw those marooned apartment towers.

✳[✳]✳

Josh was waiting for us when we got back to our rooms, his hands squirming behind his back as if he was practicing how to escape from handcuffs. It was the first time I'd seen him nervous. My grandmother invited him out to the balcony and ordered iced tea from room service. She sounded like someone from an old black and white movie. I realized she was making a conscious effort to sound like that.

The problem, Josh told us, was that my mother had escaped from police custody. My grandfather just about blew a gasket when he heard that, but my grandmother told him to calm down, indicating me with her eyes—as if his little tantrum in front of me was worse than the news itself!

I told Josh I was less worried for me than I was for my grandparents, because my mother had threatened their lives. He said he understood that, but wanted us all to rest assured. He said she wasn't likely to be much of a threat. He pulled out a blurry photograph of my mother, taken through a windshield. Her hair was bleached and permed, but there was no mistaking her. Josh said the photo had been taken at the border.

"With Mexico?" I asked. Josh nodded.

"Coming or going?"

"Going," he said.

"That poor country!" I said. Josh laughed. He said that the border police had my mother's information. They had standing instructions to arrest her if she ever tried to cross back into the States.

"Good riddance," my grandfather said.

"Amen," my grandmother said. In their minds, everything was settled.

"There are plenty of ways across a border," I said, and I was right, too. All it took was wanting it bad enough. Just look at Silvia. Or me, with my father.

But the grown-ups had spoken. I was back to being irrelevant. Josh thanked my grandmother for the tea and got up to leave. He asked me if I'd walk him to the door.

When it was just the two of us out in the hallway, he said, "I want you to try to take it easy. And call me if you need to. For any reason. It doesn't have to be an emergency." He handed me his business card, which for some reason smelled even more like barbershop powder than the rest of him. I pressed the card to my forehead, pretending to memorize it through telepathy. I wanted to tell him how incredibly much he reminded me of my father, but that would have been inappropriate, so instead I asked him to sign my cast. I gave him my cast-signing Sharpie. Without complaining or making a joke, he steadied my elbow and wrote his name on the plaster, right next to Silvia's.

"Don't throw this away," he said, tapping the cast. "Someday it may be worth something."

"Or not," I said.

"Here's your pen back," he said. "I'm serious about you calling me. Even if it's the middle of the night." He was trying to wrap things up, but I knew he wouldn't go until I said it was okay to.

It would have been childish to stand there all night enjoying my power over him, so I finally dismissed him with a dry peck on the cheek. Things got a little dreamy after that. The hallway seemed to extend like a telescope as Josh walked away, waving without looking back. The thick hotel carpet swallowed his footsteps. I waited until I heard the elevator come for him. Then I went back inside, closing the door behind me as gently as I could. When I let go of the doorknob, the automatic lock clapped shut. It startled me. Loud noises will still do that, even though I know they're coming.

Matthew Olshan is a freelance writer and producer. A native of Washington, DC, he was educated at Harvard, Johns Hopkins, and Oxford Universities. He lives in Baltimore, Maryland with his wife and daughter. *Finn: a novel* is his first published work of fiction.

"Thoroughly enjoyable and very well-written … I found myself laughing out loud on many occasions!"—*Jill Lamar, Director, Barnes & Noble's Discover Great New Writers program*

"Strap on your safety belt, there's no time to stop once you've joined 'life on the run' in this fast-paced, action-packed adventure… Although *Finn: a novel* battles stereotyping and prejudice, the reader will be satisfied with the positive ending." —*Hannah Pickworth, Middle School Librarian, Roland Park Country School*

"Like Twain's *Huckleberry Finn*, Olshan's *Finn: a novel* is both a thrilling story and a social document. Every child will enjoy it—and every adult will learn from it." —*Jesse Norman, founder/board chairman of Widelearning, an e-learning company*

"It's a great story, funny and fast-paced, concise and clear, and Chloe is one of the more lively and endearing characters I've read in some time."—*Stephen Dixon, two-time National Book Award fiction finalist*

"With remarkable skill and a modern plot, Matthew Olshan beautifully captures the lively and exciting world of Mark Twain on several levels."—*Ruth F. Boorstin, poet, children's newspaper columnist, and book editor*

"An engaging, vivid, and wonderful story!"—*Trudi Rishikof, former communications director, RI Department of Education*

"*Finn: a novel* will be very appealing to teenage as well as adult readers."—*Paul Barrett, Academic Dean, St. Albans School for Boys (Washington, DC)*

"I finished reading *Finn: a novel* last night and I couldn't help but be impressed with Matthew Olshan's writing. He certainly has created a resourceful character in Chloe. I also couldn't help but feel a bit sad that more than 100 years after *Huckleberry Finn* was originally published, the prejudices and ignorance portrayed in that novel remain on full display. Chloe is just as surprised as Huck to find that Silvia and other minorities are fully realized human beings. This book begs to be read and discussed."—*Deborah Taylor, former president of the Young Adult Library Services Association (YALSA) of the American Library Association*

"The protagonist is a teenage girl whose sense of moral responsibility and social injustice leads her to confront disquieting aspects of American society."—*Eleanor W. Kingsbury, former head of the Bermuda High School for Girls*

"It took me just a single day of my Thanksgiving holiday to ride through this fast-paced, scenic series of unforgettable adventures."—*Chloe LeGendre (13)*

"Any time I gave the slightest thought to putting down *Finn: a novel*, even for a couple of minutes, something new, exciting, and interesting happened, and I just had to keep right on reading."—*Stacy Cooper (13)*